Elementary
Drive
1

W9-AXR-466

# Calling Me Home

PATRICIA HERMES

The author wishes to thank the many who helped in the research and fact-finding for this novel, in particular, the staff of the Papillion Public Library in Papillion, Nebraska, who provided valuable texts as well as copies of original journals made by women who had settled the Nebraska territories. Ms. Sharon Wiegert, youth services librarian for the Papillion Public Library, helped provide visits to historical sites, tours of museums, and many other aids in this research. Thank you!



AVON BOOKS, INC.
1350 Avenue of the Americas
New York, New York 10019


Interior design by Kellan Peck
Visit our website at **http://www.AvonBooks.com**
ISBN: 0-380-97451-7



Library of Congress Cataloging in Publication Data:

Hermes, Patricia.
Calling me home / by Patricia Hermes.
p. cm. —(An Avon Camelot book)
Summary: Twelve-year-old Abbie struggles to accept her father's desire to make a new home for his family on the Nebraska prairies of the late 1850s.
[1. Frontier and pioneer life—Nebraska—Fiction. 2. Fathers and daughters—Fiction. 3. Christian life—Fiction. 4. Nebraska—Fiction.] I. Title.
PZ7.H4317Cal 1998 98-7909
[Fic]—dc21 CIP
AC

First Avon Camelot Printing: December 1998



Printed in the U.S.A.

OPM 10 9 8 7 6 5 4 3 2

For my son, Matthew Edward Hermes,
and his wife, Carmen Williamson Hermes,
with love.

# One

I KNOW lots of stories, mostly because Papa is always reading to us, reading from the Bible or from the other books he has there in the chest by the fireplace. At night, when he's home and work is done, he calls us all to him—Mamma and me and my sister, Sarah, and our brothers, Charlie and Nathaniel—and he reads. Certain stories, like the ones from the Bible, he reads over and over. Other stories he makes up out of his own head, but each time he tells them, they're a little bit different. One of the things Papa is always telling us is that stories help us understand our lives.

Papa has lots of sayings like that.

Now, though, I have my own story to tell, but I'm not going to just tell it. I'm going to write it.

* * *

I bent over my notebook, squinting my eyes almost shut against the hot June sun, then looked at Sarah, lying beside me. She was flat on her back, her skirt full out around her, her narrow, bony feet bare, her face tilted up to the sun. Her arms were crossed behind her head to make a pillow, and her cornhusk doll, Emmaline, was tucked under her head, too.

"I'm writing a history," I said, "a family history."

Sarah didn't answer. She just lay there, her face turned up.

I returned to my book, shielding it from the sun, leaning so I made my own shadow, and my head loomed large and dark against the page. "Did you hear, Sarah?" I said again. "Did you hear what I'm doing?"

Sarah pulled Emmaline out from under her head and folded her into her arms. She looked over at me. "I heard you, Abbie," she said.

I made a face at her. "So why didn't you answer?" I said.

"I was thinking," she said.

"That's all you ever do," I said. "How come you think so much? What are you always thinking about?"

Sarah shrugged. "Things," she said.

"What things?" I said.

Sarah smiled at me then, her face lighting up in that slow, gentle way she has. "The wind," she said. "I was thinking about the wind and how the grass must feel when the wind moves it. And how happy

I am that Mamma let us come out here today and didn't make us help in the soddy. And I was thinking about snakes and wondering why God made them." She frowned. "Why did He, do you think?"

"Why?" I said. "Because . . . just because."

"You sound like Papa," she answered. She imitated Papa's voice, gentle and soft. "Winds blow because they blow. Stars shine because they can. Bears kill because they're bears."

"Papa's right!" I said. "All those things are true. Now why are you doing that?"

Sarah had turned Emmaline in her arms, lifting her so that the sun was full on the doll's wrinkled little face.

She blinked at me. "Emmaline's cold," she said.

I started to say, Emmaline's a doll! But I didn't. With what Sarah's been through this past winter—three whole months with influenza and then the whooping cough, so sick we thought for a time she was going to die—well, maybe she needs to act like a baby for a while. At least, that's what Papa says. And who knows? Maybe Sarah was right, and Emmaline did need to be warmed through.

"So what's a family history?" Sarah said.

"A true story," I answered, "about us. All the family stories."

Sarah hugged Emmaline to her. "About us on the prairie?" she said. "Or before, when we lived in St. Joseph?"

"Both," I said. "About St. Joseph, when we had a house and a real school—good things like that.

And then about what it's like here on the prairie. In our old gopher hole."

"It's not a gopher hole, Abbie!" Sarah said, frowning the way she always does when I call it a gopher hole. "That's not nice."

Is too a gopher hole, I said, but I didn't say it out loud, just inside my head.

"Papa's building us a house," Sarah went on, still frowning. "A room, anyway. He is, and you know it."

"I know," I said, and I felt guilty for complaining. But I did long for our old house. I hated living practically underground, in a sod house made out of the earth, with a ceiling that leaked and dropped dirt and dust into our dinner. And bugs! Heavens, there were bugs, and now that it was summer, flies. And all of us jammed in just one room, to sleep, eat, and everything else, for over a year now. One year and three months, to be exact. "It's taking very much too long," I said.

"Papa said maybe by winter he'd have one room ready," Sarah said.

"That's what he said last winter," I said.

Besides, I wanted more than just a room, so much more. There was one thing in particular I missed and wished for so much. Papa always says, if wishes were horses, beggars would ride. But I couldn't help wishing. For a very long time, I'd even been saving up money. Every time Grandfather or someone sent birthday money, I put some of it in my little velvet bag.

Neither of us said anything for a minute, and then Sarah said, "Abbie?"

"What?"

"The piano?" she said.

I reached out and tugged gently on one of her braids. "Think you're a mind reader," I said.

But I smiled. Sarah reminds me so much of Papa sometimes—she hears what you don't say, hears it as clear as if you do say it.

"Yes!" I said, sighing. "It's selfish. Mamma told me it was, and she always tells me I should pray to get over being selfish and be satisfied with my lot. Well, I do pray, but you know what? I keep wishing we didn't have to sell my piano. And I can't help wanting it back!"

"Maybe someday you'll get another one," Sarah said, "an even better one! Maybe someday Papa will bring one out and surprise you."

"Out here?" I said. "How could we have a piano in our gopher hole? And what would we do when it rained and the piano got wet, just like everything else gets wet?"

"It's not a gopher hole," Sarah muttered.

"Anyway," I said, "you know all Papa's money is going to the land sale."

"But someday, maybe," Sarah said, "maybe after Papa saves enough money for the land and builds that room?" But even she didn't sound convinced.

Neither of us said anything for a while. Then Sarah said, "There's good things happening, Abbie. Like Papa told us a teacher is coming to the prairie."

"Yes!" I said. "That's good. And Papa says she's a real teacher, too, not like Mrs. Cartwright. I don't know why Papa thought Mrs. Cartwright could teach us reading this past winter when she's so dumb."

Sarah stared at me for a moment. "Abbie!" she said, softly. "You say outrageous, horrible things!"

"Well, she is dumb, don't you think?" I said. "Remember that day she didn't even know who Galileo was?"

Sarah shrugged. "Well," she said, "maybe she's not—just not very smart. Anyway, I wonder what our new teacher will be like."

"Brave," I said. "Imagine, homesteading all by herself—she and her sister—right out here on the prairie!"

"With no husbands!" Sarah said. "But I think they might have to live in town. I don't think they'll be allowed to homestead."

"They'll be allowed," I said. "Maybe they'll claim to be widows or something. I heard Papa tell Mamma that people do that sometimes."

"Are they widows?" Sarah asked.

I shook my head. "No," I said. "Papa said no."

"Then they wouldn't lie," Sarah said. "Teachers wouldn't lie. And you know what I think, Abbie? I think they must be as strong hearted and brave as you."

I smiled inside myself. But all I said was, "Do you think they might have a piano?"

"Maybe!" Sarah said. "And books, too. And maybe there'll be other children, lots of them, just like there used to be in our school in St. Joseph. Papa says the tax money is to educate all the prairie children." Sarah tilted her head. "Do you think they will build us a real school? A wooden one, like we had before?"

"No," I said, sighing. "I don't think so. It'll probably be another gopher hole."

"Abbie?" Sarah said. "Do you really hate it out here?"

"It's all right," I said, "most times."

"It's important for us, Abbie," Sarah said. "We can have land if we stay here!"

"You mean the boys can have land," I said.

"That's what I meant!" Sarah said.

That's what everybody meant. And it wasn't fair.

Papa and Mamma never once said it was unfair. I don't think they even thought it. Over and over, back in St. Joseph, Papa—and Mamma, too—kept telling us why we were moving to the prairie. "It's the only way, children," Papa had said. "The only way a man of my position can be sure to provide for his sons. If we move to the prairie, live there, prove out, pay for the land, then the boys will have land. They'll have a start, a beginning. When I'm gone, the boys will be all right."

But what about us, Papa? That's what I wanted to say. What about Sarah and me? Girls can't get land; they don't even want it—well, I don't want it. So why should we have to be out here and give up all our nice things in town? But, of course, I never said it out loud, only inside my head. I couldn't even say it to Sarah, because she'd be horrified, just like Mamma and Papa would be.

"I like it here all right," I said now. "I even love some things about it—like the way we can be free, like out here all alone today. And I can ride Maggie and have her pull the wagon. I even like the Indians—so wild and all. But I want other things sometimes. Don't you, Sarah?"

Sarah sighed. "I suppose it's wicked to want things," she said softly, "but I do."

"What do you want?" I said. "And you couldn't be wicked if you tried."

She didn't answer for a time, but after a bit, she smiled at me. "If I tell you what I want," she said, "you won't tell anyone?"

"Who would I tell?" I said. "There's not another person within miles to tell anything to!"

"Nathaniel and Charlie," she said. "You might tell them."

"Charlie!" I said. "He's just a baby! And you know I won't tell Nathaniel. He acts like an old man, like he thinks he's a papa. And he's only ten, two years younger than me, even!"

"All right then," she said, and she turned to me with this dreamy look. "I want a cat," she said, "a tiny, soft kitten, not one of those wild things. I really want one. I'd keep him in my bed and I'd let you hold him. I even pretend sometimes that I have a cat. I've already named him. His name is Fluffy."

I laughed. "What if he turns out to be not fluffy?"

"Oh, he'll surely be fluffy," she said.

"And that's all you want?" I said. "A kitten?"

"I guess I want for Papa to be home more," she said. "I wish he didn't have to stay in town. I so much miss him, when weeks and weeks go by! And I'm afraid that . . ." She paused, looking at me. "You know, don't you?" she went on. "You worry about the same thing, don't you?"

I nodded. "Say it," I said, "and I'll tell you if it's the same thing."

"I asked you first," she said.

"Did not!" I said. "I asked you first."

"All right," she said, and she took a deep breath. "Papa's worried. He told Mamma that even though we can prove out, he doesn't have enough money to buy the land yet. And he doesn't know if he can get it by land-sale time."

I nodded. "I know," I said. "I heard that, too."

"But we did prove out," Sarah said.

I nodded again. We did that.

Proving out meant you had to prove you could homestead, that you had made a home on the prairie. You had to prove that you lived in it, that you had dug a well, and that the house was at least twelve feet by fourteen feet, and even swear your house had a window. All of that we'd done, although the window wasn't much, just a frame with a bit of glass, stuck into the front wall.

But the next part was harder. Because after you proved out, there was a land sale—and you had to pay for the land. I had heard Papa say it would cost one dollar and twenty-five cents an acre—or maybe more. And with our claim at 160 acres—well, how was Papa going to get that kind of money? He worked hard building the town, only coming home to us one day every few weeks when he could get a ride on someone's wagon. Or when the weather wasn't too bad, he'd walk. Still, we never seemed to save much.

Sometimes, way deep inside me, I couldn't help hoping we wouldn't have enough money so we could move back to St. Joseph. And then I'd pray to get over feeling that way. Besides, if Papa couldn't buy this land, I was pretty sure he'd try again, and maybe we'd have to move farther west. Mamma would surely urge him to do that. I sometimes think Mamma wants land even more than Papa does.

"I heard Mamma tell him to borrow," Sarah said. "But he said not ever."

"Oh, no!" I said. "Papa wouldn't do that."

I stood up and tucked my notebook into my apron pocket. "Come on, Sarah," I said. I bent and took her hand, pulling her to her feet. "Let's get on home. Mamma gave us time off today, but she'll want us back now. She'll probably say we've been gone too long already."

Sarah got up, and we turned toward home.

We had been walking quietly awhile when Sarah suddenly turned away from me. She stepped onto a little hillock and looked out across the prairie, one hand shading her eyes from the sun, the other hugging Emmaline.

I knew what she was doing. “Silly!” I said. “You’re not going to see the teacher coming.”

“Something’s out there!” she said, pointing.

“Prairie grass,” I said, “and buffalo chips.”

But I couldn’t resist looking with her. Because, truth was, I’d been looking, too, every chance I got for the last few weeks, ever since Papa’d told us.

There was nothing to see out there, though, not yet. No small black spot creeping on the horizon. No wagon, no horses, no cattle, no dust. Nothing but prairie grass and some slow-moving dots that were buffalo.

Not yet. But I knew there would be. Papa had said so. And Papa never says what he does not mean.

# Two

IT WAS late in the day, but still hours before sunset, when Sarah and I came up to our soddy.

It had rained hard the night before, and it had rained a fair bit inside our soddy, too. Mamma and Nathaniel had dragged everything outside to dry. The beds, blankets, and mattresses, even the table and the big chest, were outside in the sun, looking strange and out of place, like the abandoned tables and chests we'd seen on the prairie trail last year. Even Papa's books, always wrapped carefully and laid inside the chest to keep dry, were lying in the sun, pages blowing as the wind dried them.

"Oh, no!" Sarah said when she saw the books. "Poor Papa!"

"They'll dry," I said. "Won't be the first time."

"Well, it's about time, you two!" Mamma said.

She had both hands on her hips, her head tipped to one side. You could see she was annoyed, but not at the really mad stage yet. Mamma gets mad much faster than Papa, especially lately, and especially at me. I think I'm a real cross to Mamma.

"It was pretty out there this afternoon, Mamma," I said. "We just walked and talked."

"And forgot the berries," she said sharply.

"Berries?" Sarah said.

I stared at Mamma, then clapped one hand over my mouth. "I forgot!" I whispered. "I clean forgot."

"And where's the bucket?" Mamma said. "You didn't lose that, did you?"

I shook my head. The bucket was still in the shed. I had gotten so excited when Mamma'd said we could have some play time that I had completely forgotten she'd also said we should come back with berries. Mamma was right—I was selfish and self-centered!

"No, Mamma," I said. "I didn't lose it. I didn't even take it. Mamma, I'm sorry."

"And Mamma promised us pies!" Nathaniel said to me. "How can she make pies without berries?"

He looked at Mamma and me, squinting against the sun. Nathaniel is very fair, his skin freckled, and the sun has bleached his hair and eyebrows so pale that sometimes he looks like he has no eyebrows at all. He's just two years younger than me and two years older than Sarah, but he always tries to act like he's the papa. He was frowning now, his eyebrows pulled together, trying to seem stern. But he wasn't any better at being firm and stern than our papa was, and as I glared back at him, I could see him beginning to smile.

"Nate, stop glaring," I said. "We forgot, that's all."

I hurried across the yard to Mamma and put my hand on her arm. "Mamma," I said, "we'll go right now. We'll go right this minute and get them."

"Well, hurry," Mamma said, "and take Charlie and watch out for him! Nathaniel and I have to round up the cow. Heather's gotten off her tether again."

"Mamma?" I said, still holding her arm and looking up into her face, browned from the sun. "Mamma, are you really going to make pies?"

"Planning on it," Mamma said. "Till you two came back empty-handed."

"We'll go get the berries now!" I said. "But really pies! With sugar?"

Mamma shook off my hand. "Go on, now," she said.

"Mamma?" I persisted. "Please, just tell me—are we expecting company? Is Papa coming?"

"Get on with you!" Mamma said. She waved her hands at me, shooing me off. But there was a soft look around her mouth, as if she was going to smile—so it must be Papa!

I knew I could tease her some when she was in this kind of mood. "We are, aren't we, Mamma?" I said. "Tell me true."

"I'll tell you true," Mamma said, "with a swift smack."

She reached out to swat me, but it was playful, and I quickly ducked out of her reach.

If Mamma was using sugar, we were expecting company! It had to be Papa. He must have found a ride out to us.

But . . . but could it also be the teacher and her sister? I turned and looked at Sarah, and she smiled at me.

"Get the bucket, Sarah," I said. "I'll get Charlie."

"You take care of him now!" Mamma called to me. "Don't let him get lost or let a snake get him! If you can get so addled you forget the berries, heaven knows what else you'll forget."

"I won't forget Charlie, Mamma," I said.

I turned to Charlie, who was crawling around on a pile of mattresses, rolling himself over and over like a baby raccoon. I reached down and gathered him into my arms. His body is warm and firm, and when I hold him, I can't help kissing him all over his sweet round face.

He put his little hands in my hair, then ran them down my face. "Obie," he said. "Obie, Obie."

He meant *Abbie,* I knew. "That's right," I said. "Abbie. Now come on, let's go."

He stuck his fingers into my mouth.

"Stop it, silly," I said, turning my face away from him.

"Obie," he said again. He looked around and grinned at Sarah, showing his two bottom teeth and four top ones. "Arah," he said.

"Yes, Sarah," I told him.

I put him on my hip, and turned to Sarah. She picked up the bucket, and together we started for the creek bed that runs behind the house, as Mamma and Nathaniel headed off the other way.

"Now remember to keep an eye on Charlie!" Mamma called. "And watch out for snakes."

"We will, Mamma," I said.

I waited just another minute, till I was sure we were out of Mamma's hearing, then turned to Sarah. "We're having company!" I said.

Sarah nodded. "If Mamma's using sugar, we are."

"Papa!" I said. "She uses sugar for Papa."

Sarah nodded. "Papa. And maybe the schoolteacher and her sister. New neighbors." She breathed deeply. "Maybe it's all of them together. I wonder where the teacher's claim will be."

"Close, I hope," I said. "Neighbors!"

We had gone only a short way when we found a large bunch of blackberry bushes with fine ripe berries, and I bent and set Charlie down, making sure first there were no snakes about.

"Stay here, don't move, little one," I told him. I kissed him on top of his head, feeling his hair, soft and fluffy. "Now don't go anywhere." I gave him a stick to play with, showing him how to draw lines in the dirt.

He grabbed the stick, and started chewing on it right away.

Sarah and I started picking, filling the bucket quickly. But after a few minutes, we had cleaned off all the bushes close to us.

"You watch Charlie, Sarah," I said. "I'll go deeper in here."

"All right," Sarah said. She picked up another stick and began drawing pictures for him in the dirt.

I went farther into the bushes, carrying the bucket. It was nasty in there, bugs swarming around my face and prickers snatching at my legs, but I kept going. If we were having company—and real pies—I wanted to be sure we had enough berries.

The bucket was almost full, when I heard Sarah calling to me.

"Abbie?" she said. "Come on back. You must have enough by now. There's mosquitoes here. I'm all bit up."

"Just one minute," I said, because I had found another treasure trove.

I continued up a little hillock, picking the biggest, juciest berries I could get my hands on. I was deep in the bushes, when I suddenly realized that I had been climbing to the very top of the ravine.

The prairie stretched out around me, flat and open and windswept, miles of prairie, miles and miles of grass rippling in the wind. And sky that came right down to meet the earth so it was like standing inside an upside-down blue cup. This wasn't a real hill or anything, not like we had in Missouri. Still, on this tiny rise, I felt as if I could see forever.

I stood for a moment, shading my eyes against the sun.

And then I saw something moving. It wasn't a mirage, wasn't my imagination, wasn't just waving grass. It was dust rising on the prairie. Wagons? Cattle? What?

I squinted into the sun.

"Abbie?" Sarah called again. "Come on back."

"Come up here, Sarah!" I called. "Bring Charlie. Come up here quick!"

In just a minute, I heard her, breaking her way through the bushes behind me, heard her feet slipping and sliding.

"Do you need a hand?" I called. "Is Charlie all right?"

"We're all right," she said. "What is it?"

She was coming up the little ravine behind me, and I reached out a hand and helped her till she was standing right alongside me. Then I took Charlie from her arms and settled him on one hip, kissing him firmly on his little fat cheek.

"Look out there!" I said.

She looked where I was pointing and frowned. "What?" she said.

"There," I said. I tucked Charlie more firmly into my hip. Then I put my hand on her chin, turning her head so she was looking where I was looking.

"I don't see anything," she said. Then she suddenly breathed out, like a little sigh. "Dust!" she said. "I see dust!"

"Something moving," I said.

She turned to me. "Buffalo?"

I shrugged. "Could be."

Sarah looked back over the prairie. “Horses, maybe,” she said. “It could be Indians.”

“Could be,” I said again.

“I think it’s a wagon with Papa,” Sarah said, “and the teacher and her sister.”

I nodded. “Yes,” I said. “That’s exactly what I think.”

# Three

IT TOOK a long while, and when night finally came down in its slow, blue-black way and the prairie sky began to wink bright with stars, whatever had been coming still hadn't arrived.

We were ready, though. Mamma had made the pies, with real sugar, and all of us had helped get things back in order in the soddy. Mamma had finally told us she was expecting Papa. A rider going past before daybreak, before any of the rest of us were awake, had told her that a wagon was on its way out, and Papa was on the wagon. I knew why she hadn't told us earlier. Things often go wrong on the prairie—wagons break down, horses and oxen fall, Indians get up to mischief. But now that we had seen the dust rising, Mamma saw fit to tell us.

I could see how excited Mamma was. After supper, she let me brush out her hair, and then she plaited it into a long braid that she wound around her head. She put on a fresh apron, too, and then she began rubbing some bear grease into her hands and arms, trying to soften them.

"Mamma?" I said, watching as she massaged her hands, hands almost as brown as the Indian women we sometimes saw. "Mamma, do you mind not having all the nice things you had back in St. Joseph?"

Mamma only pinched her lips tight and didn't answer.

Charlie was crawling around on the floor, trying to eat the bug he had grasped in his fat little hand. I picked him up and snatched the bug away. "Drop that!" I said. "That's nasty."

I turned to Mamma again. "Mamma?" I said. "I mean things like hand creams and pretty dresses and bonnets. Do you?"

Mamma turned, looking me full in the face. "Pretty is as pretty does," she said. "And don't you ever forget that."

"Yes, Mamma," I said. Even though I wasn't exactly sure what that meant. "But I mean, don't you miss—"

"No, I don't miss!" Mamma said. "This is a choice your papa and I made a year and a half ago. Both of us. It's a good decision for the whole family. And we're satisfied with it. Yes, our life is difficult sometimes. Whose life isn't?"

I didn't answer.

"Tell me that," Mamma said. "Whose life isn't difficult?"

I looked up at her. "Nobody's, Mamma," I said. "I guess."

Mamma nodded sharply, but she didn't say anything more. She just reached out and took Charlie from my arms, then started out into the yard. At the door, she stopped. "You'll be a lot happier when you learn to be content," she said softly. "Be content with your lot—all the time, not just sometimes. It's something you might pray about. And don't you go bothering your papa about 'nice things' when he gets home. You have plenty of nice things right out here. God-given things."

And she went out into the yard.

I followed her, feeling sad. I had made Mamma mad. Again. And all I had done was ask a plain old question. But she was right—I should pray. It's not right to be so filled with discontent.

I followed Mamma to the fence and stood looking across the prairie, in the direction we'd seen the dust cloud. It was cooler out here, not much, but so much better than in the soddy. I could feel the excitement in all of us. Sarah was walking all around the yard with Emmaline, pretending to show her the stars, turning her face up to the sky and pointing out the constellations that Papa had taught us. It seemed like her strength and energy were maybe coming back at last. All those months of flu and whooping cough had been hard on her.

Nathaniel had given up trying to be grown-up

and like Papa. He was running about the yard, chasing the chickens, until finally Mamma called him to settle down and let the hens be.

Me, I was more than excited. I love Papa so much. Sometimes I think I'm his favorite, more than Nathaniel—even though papas are supposed to favor their sons. When I'm alone with Papa, we talk about things, things I could never talk about with Mamma. Last time he was home, I'd told him I knew I was pretty and that I liked pretty things, and he didn't get mad. I said that when I grew up, I'd live in a real house in town. I'd have sweet little girl children and dress them all in pretty clothes, but I'd let them run free too, the way we run on the prairie. I'd even let my little girls ride horses. And then Papa had looked sad, and that worried me, so I told him that maybe I'd have one boy, too, and Papa had just laughed. He hadn't gotten mad.

Just then, I heard the sounds of hooves and something heavy rolling. And there it was, coming into sight, rolling across the plains—the strangest sight I had ever seen.

We all rushed to the fence and stared at what was approaching. I looked at Mamma, then turned back to stare some more. It was a wagon, a huge flat wagon, pulled by an ox team. On the wagon . . . I blinked.

On the wagon was a *house.* A complete house. It was small—a log house with a window and a door—an entire house moving across the prairie.

And on the wagon, waving to us, were some men.

And there among them—Papa. Papa bringing us a house!

"Papa!" I cried.

All of us—Nathaniel and Sarah and me—ran from the yard. We ran across the prairie to the wagon and then turned and crowded alongside it as it slowly rolled to a stop by our fence. Papa jumped down and went right by us, with just a touch for each of our heads, and over to Mamma.

He swept her into his arms, held her close, and Charlie, too. And then, right there in front of everybody, he gave her a big kiss, and she didn't pull away. And then Papa took Charlie from her and held him close, snuggling his face to Charlie's.

Charlie hadn't seen Papa in weeks and weeks, and he began to wail and howl, the way he'd done that time an Indian woman had lifted him. He leaned out of Papa's arms, reaching for Mamma and wailing.

"A real mamma's baby!" Papa said, but he was laughing.

He handed Charlie back to Mamma, then turned to us, his arms out. Nathaniel was first into his arms, and then Sarah. Papa held them close, whispering to them, while I held back. I always wait to be hugged last, because that way, I get the longest hugs of all.

"Papa," I whispered, when it was my turn and Papa had brought me in and was holding me close. "Papa! Oh, Papa. You brought us a house! Thank you, thank you. A real house."

Papa held me away, smiling down at me. "No!"

he answered. "No, no, no." He put a finger under my chin and turned my face so I was looking at the house. "How would we fit in that little thing?" he asked quietly.

I turned back, puzzled. It wasn't that small, not much smaller than our soddy. "Then what's it for?" I said.

"It's just something I hitched a ride home on," Papa said, holding me close again. "They were coming out from town, and they let me come along. When we're settled, I'll tell you all about it."

"But then . . . it's not ours?"

"No, it's not ours," Papa said.

I could feel tears rise to my eyes, and I pressed my face hard against his chest. I had hoped! I had really, really hoped. A house, maybe with room for a piano someday.

But then, another thought began forming, a good one. If it wasn't for us, maybe it was for the schoolteacher and her sister.

"Papa?" I said, pulling away. "Papa, is it for the teacher? Are we getting new neighbors?"

Papa raised his eyebrows at me, then slowly shook his head, smiling. "Not yet," he said. "It's not for the teacher."

"Oh," I said. I looked over at the house.

Papa patted my head. "My dear girl," he said, "one of these days, you'll have the best house on the prairie—you wait and see. But this house isn't for anyone. It's just a house. I'll tell you all about it later. Now it's time to get settled in."

Papa let go of me, then turned to the team driver and the other men on the wagon, and all of them began unhitching the oxen, leading them to a spot with water and grass, where they could be tethered for the night. I didn't recognize any of the other men, but we were used to having strangers stop, since we were the first homestead on the prairie, fifteen miles outside Grand Island. Mamma always offered food and a place to sleep to anyone who came by. Sometimes people paid, and sometimes they didn't, but Mamma fed everyone.

Now, Nathaniel went running for some water buckets to help Papa, and I looked around at Sarah and Mamma.

Mamma was smiling, but Sarah looked as puzzled as I felt. She'd been standing close enough to hear what Papa had said to me. Now, she came even closer and slid her hand into mine.

"The house isn't for us," she whispered, although why she was whispering, I didn't know.

"No, not for us!" I answered.

"And not for the teacher and her sister," she added.

"I know," I said. "Not for them, either, Papa said."

Sarah leaned against me. "Know what I thought at first?" she said. She stood up on tiptoe and whispered right in my ear. "I thought it was a dollhouse for us and for Emmaline and Fluffy," she said.

I couldn't help smiling at her. "Silly!" I said.

"Come, girls," Mamma called from behind us.

"Let's get food for Papa and the men. And, Abbie, you come and put Charlie to bed."

Sarah and I followed Mamma into the soddy, Sarah turning once to look back at the house.

Inside, Sarah went to help Mamma with the table, while I took Charlie from Mamma's arms.

I carried him to his corner bed near the fireplace, a small boxlike cradle with sides high enough to keep him from falling out and to keep snakes from getting in—though snakes could get in anywhere if they really wanted to. One had done just that last fall, and had bitten Charlie, and it had taken the Indians to tell Mamma what herbs to use to make him well. We'd all been terrified of snakes ever since.

I lay him down in his bed and covered him with a tiny scrap of sheet. It was awful hot in here, too hot for covers, but he always needs to hold on to something when he sleeps.

Most nights, he howls if he's put to bed before the rest of us. But this night he was so tired he settled to sleep almost before I covered him. His little thumb went right to his mouth, and in just seconds, I could hear him slurping away at it.

I stood by, crooning to him awhile, thinking about a night prayer for him. It's something Papa taught us—to pray for one another every night, to tell God what we wish for others, always to think of others, every single night. I stood over Charlie, thinking about what I was supposed to pray for, but other thoughts kept getting in the way. How could Papa bring us a perfect little house—and not let us use it? What was he up to? And where were the teacher and the neighbors? When were they coming?

I looked over my shoulder at Mamma humming and tending the fire, at Sarah busily laying the table, bringing out the bread—the pies!—neither of them seeming at all bothered by the house that wasn't ours. I turned back to Charlie, took a deep breath, and closed my eyes. Dear God, I prayed . . .

Whose house is it then?

I squinched up my eyes even tighter. Dear God, let Charlie never meet a snake again. Let him live to grow up. Let him like to read when he grows up. . . .

Why did they build the house first, and then carry it here?

And God, let Charlie be a big help to Papa when he grows up. God, make him be smart, because then, if we don't stay on the prairie, he can get work for himself and . . .

I opened my eyes and looked down at him sleeping. I watched his eyelids twitch. Was he dreaming already? What did babies dream?

I looked around me once more—at Mamma, at Sarah, at Papa and Nathaniel and the men beginning to crowd in at the door, all of them laughing, busy, looking happy. Mamma was bent over the stove, hot, pushing the hair off her forehead, but she was happy, I could see. Her hands fairly flew as she turned flapjacks, made coffee, preparing a meal for Papa and the men, happy to have Papa home for a while.

Happy with my lot, Abbie, I could almost hear her say.

And Papa, he was happy too, standing in the doorway, smiling that sweet smile of his. I saw him look over at me, and he held my eyes for a moment, his head tipped to one side, as if wanting to hear my thoughts.

I smiled at him, then bent my head and tried to finish my prayer.

Dear God, I prayed, dear God, let me be content. Let me be like Mamma, like Papa and Sarah and Nathaniel, happy with our lot.

I opened my eyes and looked at them all again, then looked out through the front door of the soddy, past the men gathered there, to where the perfect little house stood on its wagon in the moonlight.

I closed my eyes and took a deep breath. Dear God, I prayed again, let me be happy with my lot. But if you can, dear God, bring us one of those fine houses, too. Amen.

# Four

NEXT MORNING, the men with the wagon were gone early, off across the prairie, taking their house with them before I was even awake. Papa stayed behind with us. He had a whole week free to be home, he said, a whole week between projects in town.

The night before, I had gone to bed still not knowing about the house. Papa hadn't let any of us ask questions while the men were there, so at breakfast, it was the first thing I asked about.

"Papa?" I said. "Where is the house going? And why is it already built on a platform?"

"It's going farther on," Nathaniel said in that superior tone of voice he uses sometimes, like he's the grown-up and I'm just a little child. "It's going to a family farther on across the prairie."

"Well, I know that!" I said, wrinkling my nose at him. "Papa told me that, too."

I turned to Papa. "But what family, Papa?" I said. "Where? And why is it all built already and on a wagon?"

Papa looked at Mamma, then at Sarah and Nathaniel and me. "Actually," he said, "it's not going to a family. I hate to tell of dishonesty, but you'll hear more about things like this."

He leaned forward, his elbows on the table, looking straight at us. "Nobody's going to live in that house," he said. "Nobody."

"Nobody!" Nathaniel said. "Why not?"

"It's a sweet little house!" Sarah said. "It's beautiful. And it has a window."

"Papa!" I said. "Could we buy it, then? I mean, I know we don't have much money, but it can't cost much—it's so little. If nobody's going to live in it, could we maybe . . ."

I saw Mamma's mouth set in a straight line, and I quickly closed up my own mouth.

"No, we can't buy it," Papa said. "And nobody's going to live in it because . . . well, you see, in order to prove out, you have to swear that there's a house on your land—you know that, right? People rent that house. They pay five dollars a day for it! They do that so they can swear they have a house on their land, with a window. And after they swear to that, then the house gets moved to somewhere else."

"But that's not honest!" Nathaniel said.

"No, it's not," Papa said.

"Well, it's sort of honest," I said. "I mean if it's on their land . . ."

Papa looked at me.

"I guess not," I said. And then I added, "Papa? How about our house? If you're going to be home for a week, can we start building our new room this week? I'll help—we all will."

Papa shook his head. "Soon," he said. "But I think this week we'll work on what we already have. It's getting too hot for your mamma to have the cookstove indoors, so we'll move that out. The roof leaks, so we need to fix that. And the garden needs work. We'll think about a new room in the fall."

"But that's what you said last year!" I said.

"I know," Papa said.

"And in the fall," I said, "then you'll say—"

"Abbie!" Mamma said, her voice sharp. "That's enough."

Papa turned to Mamma and touched her arm gently. "It's all right," he said quietly. "It's all right if she wants things."

He turned back to me then. "Abbie," he said, "I know it's hard to want something and to have it put off again and again. I'll do my best, you know that."

"I know that," I said quietly. "I just thought—"

"No!" Mamma said. "You didn't think. That's your problem. You don't think. And if you do, all you think about is yourself."

"It's all right," Papa said quietly, patting Mamma's hand. "It's all right."

I looked down at Charlie, who was crawling around the floor next to me, then bent over and put a hand out to him. Well, the room wouldn't be just for me, I thought; it would be for all of us. But of course I didn't say it out loud.

I lifted Charlie onto my lap and put a hand on his soft hair, feeling the bones of his skull, the top of his head now hard and firm, that little soft spot that babies have almost all closed now.

Everyone was quiet for a minute, and I wondered what they were thinking. Sarah was smiling, a dreamy kind of smile, and I imagined her thinking about having the little house for Fluffy and Emmaline. Nate looked cheerful too, and I knew how happy he was to have Papa home, to have time with him.

And Papa—Papa was looking out toward the doorway now, his hand covering Mamma's on the table, a half smile on his face. He was happy to be home, I knew that, happy to work together.

I looked down at Charlie in my lap, Charlie who had a whole fistful of my hair twisted in his hand now, who was grinning at me, drool in one corner of his mouth.

And then I looked at Mamma. She was the only one who wasn't smiling, that pinched look still on her face—because of me, I knew.

"It's a good day to work," Papa said, patting Mamma's hand, then standing up and moving toward the door. "Outdoors first, I think. Who's ready to help me?"

"I am, Papa!" Nate and Sarah said, both at the same time.

"Sarah, you stay here and help me," Mamma said. "I don't want you working in that sun. It's going to be real hot today."

"But, Mamma!" Sarah said.

"I'll help you, Papa!" I said. "Tell me what to do."

"Roof work," he said. "We need to cut some new sod. I think that's our number one need."

"Then can I go up on the roof with you to set it in?" I said.

Papa nodded.

"Yippee!" I said.

That was one good thing about the prairie. I could do things I'd never been allowed to in town, things only boys got to do. Last year when we built the soddy, I loved the time I spent up on the roof, looking out over the prairie, Papa by my side.

Papa was smiling at me. I figured he knew exactly what I was thinking, that he knew how I loved being with him.

A wave of feeling swept over me then, and I looked over at Mamma, suddenly wanting to tell her that I was happy. That I was content. I even opened my mouth, but then I closed it again.

She wouldn't believe me. I knew she wouldn't. And if she did, she'd say I was the most contradictory person she'd ever met. She tells me that a lot. And I don't blame her.

I stood up then, and handed Charlie to Sarah, kissing the top of his head. As I did, I made a promise to Mamma, a silent promise inside my head: I would try like anything to be content, to be as happy as I was at this moment. I would try to be like Sarah and Nathaniel and Papa and Mamma herself. I'd try to forget about what I didn't have and think about what I had. I'd pray every day, asking God to help me be happy with my lot.

It was a promise. A silent one. But still, a promise.

# Five

THAT WEEK was one of the best ever. Maybe God had answered my prayers. I didn't feel sad, didn't long for something else; I was happy with my lot. Of course, I had much to be happy about, with Papa home. We worked hard, but having Papa there made it fun—listening to his stories, his songs. He would tell us to sing along with him, to make "joyful noise," as he called it. He taught us all kinds of songs—church songs and nursery rhymes, and old-time songs that his mamma had sung to him. Even without the piano, the singing seemed fine to me. We weeded our garden, repaired the roof of the soddy, brought the cookstove outside and placed it by the door, and did all the little things that needed doing.

One of the best things was that Mamma seemed

sweet to me again, the way she used to be before we came out here. Maybe it was because I was being different. Could she tell that I was content? One day, when she washed my hair, she spent a long time brushing it out, rubbing my scalp with her strong fingers. She didn't say anything, but I knew she was doing it because she knows how I love having my head massaged.

Anyway, the days were wonderful, and at night, after the work was done, it was even better. That was when Papa would read to us.

That week, he chose to read to us from the Acts of the Apostles. I lay on the ground, my eyes closed, listening, picturing all the things Papa's words brought to life. I loved the names, the way they rolled off Papa's tongue like music—Ptolemais, Agabus, Cyprus, Tyre, Judea. Musical words, lyrical words. Many nights, I fell asleep right there on the ground, listening, and felt Papa lift me and place me on my bed.

Finally, though, the week was over, the work was done, and it was time for Papa to go back to town. And then something else good happened: Nate got sick. I don't mean that it was good that Nate was sick—but the good thing was that I got to take Papa back to town. It was fifteen miles, a long hard walk for Papa, but an easy ride now that it was summer. Most times, Nathaniel's the one who gets to drive Papa in the wagon, because he's a boy. But with Nathaniel sick and fevery, Mamma said I could go.

That meant I had the long ride and all that time to talk alone with Papa. I would also be allowed to spend the morning in town, walking around, looking in stores. I couldn't wait to be in a real town, with people and shops and everything. We've only been to town a few times since we've been on the prairie—twice to buy supplies and then last summer for the Fourth of July festival.

Papa and I set out long before dawn. Mamma wanted me to buy her some needles, and I had the money tied up in a handkerchief in my apron pocket. When we were settled on our wagon, our dinner tucked in between us, Papa looked over at me, smiling.

"Well, Abbie, my girl," he said, and he clucked and moved the reins over Maggie's back. "Time for us, eh?"

I moved a little closer to him. "I'm glad you came home, Papa," I said. "I miss you when you're gone."

Papa nodded. "I know," he said. He clucked again at Maggie. "Come on, girl!" he said.

Maggie's really old and hates to get moving, especially in the morning, but finally Papa got her on her way. He settled back against the boards. "It's hard to live apart like this," he said. "But we'll be back together in time. For now, I make enough money to make it worth our while."

Enough to buy the land? I started to say, but I thought better of it. Papa always got that worried look when he talked about the land sale. Instead, I said, "When will you be able to stay with us? Stay for good?"

Papa shook his head. "Don't know, girl," he said. "Sometime soon, I hope."

"Grown-up soon or child soon?" I said.

Papa looked at me, his eyebrows up.

"You know," I said, "grown-ups say everything is soon. But grown-up soon can take a long time. Child soon is really soon."

Papa laughed. "Soon is soon, my dear," he said, "but I'll tell you what. Something very exciting is coming to the prairie. Really soon. You might even call it child soon."

"The teacher and her sister?" I said. "The one who's going to homestead?"

Papa nodded.

"How do you know they're coming soon?" I said.

"Because they're already in town. I've met them," Papa said. "It's two whole families. A Mr. and Mrs. Richardson, and Mr. Richardson's sisters. They're fine-looking people, and the one who's the teacher seems to be a right smart one."

"They're already in town and you've met them?" I said, staring at him. "You have? Why didn't you tell us before?"

"Well, no sense getting excited just yet," Papa said, smiling. "They're still getting outfitted, and you know how long that takes. They've already staked two claims, though, one for each family. I understand the first claim is just downriver from ours, maybe five miles or so. The next one is just past that."

"And children, Papa?" I said. "Are there any children?"

"At least one that I know of. Maybe two."

"Boys or girls?" I could feel myself holding my breath. A boy, please, a boy, so they'll stay. And a girl, too. To play with, please, God. Two girls would be better.

"Boys, I think," Papa said.

"Oh," I said, disappointed. "Well, at least they'll stay, then."

Papa looked at me.

I nodded. "Yes, because if it's girls, they'll not need the land. So if they don't like the prairie, if they freeze in winter or if they hate the sound of the wind all the time, or if it rains inside their soddy, they'll leave."

"Well," Papa said, "that could happen. But I have a feeling these people will stay. They seem real serious about their intentions. And, of course, the tax is paying the teacher, so she'll stay."

"Papa?" I said. "The teacher and her sister are single, you said?"

Papa nodded.

"Then how can they homestead? How can they get land for themselves? Will they pretend to be widows?"

"I don't know about that," Papa said. "But women can homestead if they're heads of household, widows or not."

"But how can single ladies be heads of household?" I said.

Papa flicked the reins over Maggie, sending a whole swarm of flies up into the air to circle our heads.

"Papa?" I said.

"Sometimes women adopt a child," Papa said, waving his arm at the flies. "That makes them head of household. Or sometimes they're left a child by a family member who dies. There's lots of ways to be head of household."

"Oh," I said. And for a long while, I didn't say anything more. I looked out over the prairie, watched the grasses wave in the soft wind, thought about all the babies who got orphaned on the way out here and about adopting and . . .

Papa reached over and touched my knee. "Abbie?" he said. "Someday, women will be allowed to have land, too. I know that day will come. Don't fret over it."

I looked at him. "I wasn't thinking about land," I said. "I mean, it's not fair that girls can't get land, but I wasn't thinking about that."

"But you're thinking something big," Papa said, smiling at me.

I couldn't help smiling back. Papa reminds me so much of Sarah at times—or maybe she reminds me of him. They both have that way of knowing what's in your head.

"Yes," I said. "I was thinking about what you said about adopting. That's what I'll do when I grow up. I don't really like any boys. So that way, I won't have to marry, but I can adopt a little baby. And I can be sure to get a girl baby, too."

For a moment, Papa looked at me, surprised.

"What?" I said.

He shook his head. Then he began to smile. And then he threw back his head and laughed and laughed. "Abbie," he said, "you are irrepressible!"

"What's that mean?" I said. "And you're laughing at me!"

Papa put a hand on my hand. "I'm not laughing at you, Abbie, girl," he said.

"You are too laughing at me," I said.

"I'm not, Abbie," Papa said, and I could see that he was trying hard not to, but there was still that shiny, laughing look in his eyes. "But you do surprise me. Besides, don't you think a child might miss not having a papa?"

"Well," I said slowly, "well, Sarah could marry—she likes boys—and then my baby could have an uncle. That would be almost like a papa."

Papa took a deep breath then, and his eyes got serious. When he spoke, his voice was serious, too. "Some people do something very evil," he said. "They adopt a child till they get land, and afterward, they send the child back."

"How awful!" I said. "I would never do that."

"I know you wouldn't," Papa said. "But it troubles me what people do, Abbie. There are so many dishonest things people are doing to get land. I told you about that house I rode out on, and—"

And then I heard Papa make a sound, like he had sucked his breath in real fast.

"What?" I said.

"Indians," Papa answered. "Horses."

"Oh!" I said.

I turned and looked where Papa was looking. There were horses coming, Indians on horses, a whole lot of them. They were coming on fast, thundering toward us, dust rising. I could suddenly feel the earth moving, even through the wagon.

I looked over at Papa. I felt my heart thudding hard in my throat.

"Are they friendly, Papa?" I said.

Papa's mouth was drawn into a tight line. "Might be," he said. "Might not."

He clicked his tongue at Maggie, flicking the reins harder across her back. Like that would do any good! Old Maggie outrun the Indians on their horses?

I looked across the plains, watching the Indians come. And then I saw something behind them—dogs, it looked like, pulling carts loaded down with wigwam sticks and lots of women and children.

"See that, Papa?" I said.

Papa nodded, seeming to relax a bit. "Just moving their village," he murmured to me. "Not up to any mischief. I hope."

And then suddenly, we were surrounded, Indians on all sides of our wagon.

Papa reined Maggie in. "Whoa, girl," he said softly.

I could feel my heart beating fast and hard. I remembered all the bad stories I had heard—of the baby who was stolen right out of a wagon, right out of his mamma's arms. I remembered the scalps the Indians carried proudly, hanging from their belts. I'd seen them myself.

I remembered the time an Indian suddenly burst inside our soddy. He'd come right up to Mamma, taken hold of her braid, and held a knife to it, and none of us knew if he'd meant to cut off her braid or to scalp her right there in front of us. But Mamma, she'd just snatched her braid back from him and given him her dark look. "Mind your manners," she'd said. That Indian, he'd backed up. But for the rest of that whole entire day, he'd stood in a corner of the soddy watching us, like he was planted there.

I remembered, too, the Indians standing in our soddy, their hands filled with herbs and brews for Charlie when he got snakebite.

Now I looked up at the Indian closest to Papa. He was staring right into Papa's face.

He was fierce looking—his face painted in stripes, his hair all bushed out, with sticks and twigs clinging to it. He was wearing practically no clothes, just a cloth hanging down from his waist.

He held out his hand to Papa, a gesture that seemed to mean he wanted to shake hands.

Papa reached out and grasped the hand of the Indian. "How do," Papa said politely.

The Indian nodded. "How," he said back.

They shook hands for a long time, looking into each other's faces, pumping their hands up and down while I waited, holding my own breath. Did the Indians want something? Should Papa offer them something? Should I? People said Indians were terrible beggars, but sometimes wasn't it that they were hungry?

Maybe I should offer them our dinner?

After a moment, the Indian nodded. "Girl," he said, looking at me. "Daughter?"

"Yes," Papa answered. "My daughter. A good girl."

I felt my heart thud even more violently. Did they want me? Were they going to steal me away, just like they'd stolen the baby?

The Indian was looking hard at me. "Good girl," he repeated.

"No!" I blurted out. "I'm not really good! I'm very bad!"

Now Papa looked at me, surprised.

The Indian let go of Papa's hand, but he kept staring at me.

"I am!" I said. "I'm very bad, and I'm selfish and lots of times I'm addle-brained, and I'm never satisfied with my lot, just ask Mamma. And you have sticks in your hair."

"Abbie!" Papa murmured. "Abbie."

"But he does, Papa!" I said. I looked at the Indian. "Are you hungry?" I said. "Want some food? Our dinner?"

I held out our dinner from the seat beside us, wrapped in one of Mamma's dishcloths.

For a long moment, the Indian kept looking at me, not speaking, not moving, just staring. I could hear the others coming nearer, could feel the movement of earth, could hear the horses all around us, stomping their hooves. I could hear and even feel their breath. All the while, that Indian just looked at me.

And then he smiled. He lifted one hand, nodded to the others on their horses, and all of them suddenly whirled their horses around. They rode away, the ground shaking under them, dust flying up as I turned to watch.

Papa flicked the reins again, and we began moving slowly.

"Papa," I whispered, "I was scared."

Papa nodded. "I'd be lying if I said I wasn't."

"What did they want, Papa?" I said. "Did they want me?"

"They didn't want you," Papa said.

"Because I told them I was bad?" I said.

Papa laughed. "Abbie," he said, "I told you before. You are irrepressible."

"Is that something bad?" I said.

"It's not an insult," Papa said.

"What's it mean?" I said.

"It means—well, it's hard to explain. But it means nothing will get you down for long. Nothing can keep you down." And then, just like before, he began to laugh. "Consider it a compliment," he said.

"Did the Indian think I was irrepressible, too?" I said.

"I don't know what he thought," Papa said. "I think he just wanted to shake my hand. But I'm sure he didn't want you."

"I'm glad," I said. Although I wasn't absolutely

sure that he hadn't at least thought of stealing me away.

"Anyway," Papa said, "for now, I'm glad they're gone."

"I am, too, Papa," I said. "I am, too."

# Six

I HAD so much looked forward to having that time alone with Papa, but once the Indians had ridden away, I was anxious to get to town. I think Papa was worried, too. Both of us had become quiet, and we spent the rest of the ride looking anxiously out over the prairie.

I had another reason for wanting to get to town. As soon as Papa had told me the teacher was there, I had made a plan: I was going to meet her. I didn't know yet how I'd arrange it, but I knew I could do it.

I smiled inside. Papa had said I was "irrepressible"—and that was good. Consider it a compliment, he'd said. I liked compliments, especially from Papa. Mamma didn't ever give me a compliment. I thanked God then that the Indian hadn't stolen me away from my family, and prayed again to try to please Mamma more, to be less addle-brained and selfish. I wondered if God got tired of me always promising that, and then in the next moment, being selfish and addle-brained again. I did mean it, though.

It took about another hour before we got to the town of Grand Island. Papa stopped the wagon, jumped down, and fastened Maggie's reins to a hitching post on the main street.

I stood up in the wagon, then straightened my skirts and underthings. "Riding in a wagon hurts your rear end, Papa," I said.

Papa laughed. "But your mamma wouldn't like to hear you use those words," he said.

"What words should I use?" I said.

Papa pursed his lips. "Don't know," he said, "actually. But I guess your mamma would say you shouldn't mention it at all."

I shrugged. "But it's a part of your body!" I said. "Everyone has one."

Papa laughed again. "That's for sure," he said.

"Anyway, it does hurt," I said. I pulled my shoes out from under the seat. They were a bit tight, but Mamma makes us wear shoes in town, even though we never wear them on the prairie until the snow falls.

When I had my shoes on, Papa reached a hand up to me, and I jumped down.

"Would you like to see where I work before I leave you?" Papa said.

"Yes," I said. "And I want to see where you live."

Papa smiled. "That will make you laugh."

"Why?" I said.

"You'll see," Papa said.

We started along the wooden sidewalk that ran the length of the street. It had been months since I'd been here, and the town had changed so much! There were so many new buildings. Some were several stories tall, and all were crowded in on top of one another. I saw a tinsmith's, a veterinary, and a cobbler's shop, two saloons, two churches, an apothecary, and the new doctor's office. It was as if the town had sprung up out of the prairie, the way prairie grass and wildflowers seem to spring up overnight once the winter is gone. There were signs everywhere, telling about the July Fourth festival, inviting people to come for the picnic and the games. It was so busy, so different from the prairie, that I felt like my head was spinning! The town was even prettier than St. Joseph, all of it so alive, so noisy and busy. One of the new sidewalks was even covered with a roof, to keep off the rain and snow.

I began counting on my fingers how many people I saw, but I gave it up in a minute. Ten? Thirty? A hundred, maybe? I had seen more people in the last few minutes than I'd seen in a month—no, a year—on the prairie.

I reached up and took Papa's hand.

"Papa?" I said. "It's so big here and so beautiful! Look at that building!" I pointed to a bank, two stories tall, with a clock on the front. "Isn't that huge?"

"That it is," Papa said. "I helped build that one. I did all the carpentering inside. And that one?"

He pointed to a place that seemed to be just a cellar. "That's what I'll be starting on this week," he said.

I nodded. Papa can do most anything with his hands—he's a carpenter and a bricklayer—which is why I wonder how come he hasn't built us a house yet.

We walked along together, hand in hand, and people stopped to say good morning. I wondered if any of them were Mr. Richardson's sisters, and which one was the teacher. I thought of asking Papa where they lived, but I thought he might tell me to mind my business. It was better not to ask, so I wouldn't be disobedient, because I had made up my mind that I was going to find out.

I began to realize that people, women especially, were smiling, like they were approving of us.

I looked up at Papa. Papa is hard and brown from working out of doors in the sun. But he's very handsome. Everybody says so, even Mamma. It felt very nice to have people looking and smiling at us, and I smiled back, nodding like I was a grown-up lady.

I turned to see our reflection in a store window. We have a mirror in the soddy, but it's just big enough to see your face and hair. Here was the complete me, from my head to my feet.

I was wearing my everyday dress, and it was awfully old, but after the winter, Mamma had let down the hem so it fit better. My shoes looked decent enough, but I realized I didn't look as nice as the townspeople. My dress was faded and kind of limp, not stiff like the dresses I saw around me. I tried to fluff out my skirt. But then I figured I looked pretty enough, and my bonnet was really sweet. And at least my dress was long, almost to my feet.

I had to smile inside. How shocked Mamma would be if she knew what I was wearing under my dress!

"Well," Papa said after a while. "How do you like the town?"

"I love it," I said, smiling up at him. "I'd love to live here, Papa." I saw a sad look come across his face, and I quickly added, "But the prairie is nice, too."

Papa squeezed my hand. "That it is," he said. "That it is."

We had reached the end of the sidewalk. We stepped off it and turned a corner, down a narrow dusty path. Then Papa stopped and pointed. "This is it," he said.

"This is what?" I said.

"This is where I live," Papa said.

"Here?" I said.

We were standing outside a house—a big house! It had two floors, with many windows and soft white curtains blowing outward in the breeze.

There was a porch that ran all around the front and two sides, and on it were chairs. The house was painted a bright white with black trim, and it had chimneys, lots of them, meaning fireplaces inside.

I looked up at Papa. "You live here?" I said. "It's so beautiful."

Papa shook his head. "Not exactly," he said. "I eat here. And I can wash up inside. It's a boardinghouse. But I actually live *here*." He pointed down at the ground in front of us.

"On the ground?" I said. "Out of doors?"

Papa nodded. "Right on the ground and out of doors. It saves money. Many men do it. We pay a few cents a week to sleep here, but we eat inside and wash up in there. So it works."

"You mean it?" I said. "You really sleep out here?"

Papa nodded.

"But Papa!" I said. "You don't even have a roof!"

Papa pointed upward. "God's roof. God's sky," he said. "A blanket of stars and God above. What more could a person want?"

"I'd want a roof!" I said.

Papa laughed and shook his head at me.

"But aren't you cold, Papa?" I said. "Or wet?"

Papa nodded. "Sometimes," he said. "But when it gets really cold, I'll find other lodgings."

He took my arm, turning me back the way we had come. "Time to go to work now," he said.

We walked back, both of us quiet. I didn't know

what Papa was thinking, but my mind was racing, thinking about the way Papa lived.

When we turned the corner and were back on the sidewalk, Papa let go of my hand. "I'll meet you at the wagon at noontime," he said. "We'll eat dinner and then you can head back home."

He reached into his pocket. "Here," he said, and pressed some coins into my hand. "I know how you love sweets. But don't tell your mamma."

I looked down. Three pennies! I could buy candy—one penny for me and one for Sarah and one for Nathaniel. There'd be none for Charlie, but he was too little to notice or care about candy, anyway.

"Thank you, Papa," I said. "Thank you. I won't tell. But can I take some candy to Sarah and Nathaniel?"

Papa raised his eyebrows. "Then your mamma will know," he said.

"Don't worry," I said. "I'll find a way."

Papa laughed. "We shouldn't sneak," he said. "But I think you deserve a treat. It was a scary morning. And don't forget to buy your mamma's needles."

"I won't forget, Papa!" I said.

Papa smiled at me and turned to go, but then he turned back. He reached in his pocket again. "And this is for you to keep," he said, and pressed a nickel into my hand.

"But you just gave me three pennies, Papa," I said.

"Yes," Papa said. "But this is to save. For your wishing bag."

I ducked my head. I never mention the little velvet bag where I've been saving money. But Papa never forgets.

"Thank you, Papa," I said.

Papa turned then and walked away, lifting a hand in a wave.

I stood on the sidewalk, watching him go, wondering, thinking.

Mamma was right—I was selfish. Papa worked so hard. He slept out of doors and he'd never even told us, never complained. He slept on the ground!

And he gave me pennies and a nickel, money that could probably buy him a night's sleep in the boardinghouse.

I didn't much love the soddy. And the roof leaked something awful. But how must it be to not even have a roof?

# Seven

I STOOD for a few minutes, thinking about Papa, feeling sad, then started off to the dry goods store.

I had gone only a few steps, though, when I began to feel better. The day was too sweet to be sad, and I had so much to do. Besides, Papa hadn't seemed sad. Maybe he didn't mind at all!

First, I'd get Mamma's needles, and then I'd have the rest of the morning to myself.

I hurried into the dry goods store, picked out the two packages of needles, and paid with the twenty-five cents that Mamma had tied up in my handkerchief.

There was a big glass display of candies in the front of the store, and I spent many minutes choosing the right ones. For Nathaniel, I chose licorice—hateful stuff, I think, but he likes it. For Sarah, hard candies. She likes them because they last the longest. And for me—fudge. Chocolate fudge. A whole square of it, all to myself. I would eat some on the way home and save some for tomorrow.

I went out onto the sidewalk and looked around. How would I find the schoolteacher?

Up ahead, I could see two women walking side by side, each with a parasol to shade her from the sun, each parasol a lovely pale blue. Their dresses were made of the same blue fabric, too, perhaps from the same bolt of cloth. Was one of them the schoolteacher? Were they sisters? Sisters might wear dresses from the same bolt of cloth, mightn't they?

But just as I decided they might be Mr. Richardson's sisters, and one might be the teacher, the women went into a store. When they turned, I saw they were really, really old, grandmother kind of old. Surely the teacher would be young.

Now what? I could ask in the stores. But I knew that shopkeepers were usually too busy to spend time talking with children. And then I remembered that behind the shops was a narrow alley where men gathered sometimes, sitting on barrels or crates, playing checkers or talking. I could go back there and ask if any of them knew about the new teacher. They wouldn't be too busy to talk.

I stepped off the sidewalk and threaded my way between the oxcarts and horses beginning to crowd the street. When I got to the corner, I headed toward the alley.

Once around the corner, I lifted my skirts and began to run. I wasn't running for any reason. I was running because I was happy, because it felt good to run, and nobody was around to tell me otherwise. I ran like I run on the prairie, chasing prairie chickens. I pretended the Indians from this morning were chasing me. I could almost feel them coming, and I turned, looking behind me.

"Watch out!" somebody yelled.

A boy had appeared in front of me, and again, he yelled, "Watch out, stop!"

But I was going too fast and I ran pell-mell, smack into him. I felt the bump and crunch as our heads met. I hit him so hard, it sent me reeling backward. I would have fallen, but his hand shot out and grabbed me by the sleeve of my shirtwaist. When he saw I wasn't going to fall, he let go.

The boy seemed to be my age, and just about my size. His face was brown and thin, and he had dark, straight hair and almost black eyes. Even though one hand covered his mouth and nose—feeling to see if his face was still in one piece, I guess—I could see he had a mean kind of look.

I put a hand to my own face. I felt a bump already rising on my forehead, and a little cut there, too, where I had slammed into his teeth. He had bitten me! For some reason, that made me feel like laughing, but I knew I shouldn't, especially the way he was looking at me.

I backed up a little. "Sorry," I said. "I didn't see you."

"I know that!" he said. He frowned at me. "Who was chasing you?"

I straightened my dress, smoothing down my skirts. "No one," I said. "I was . . . in a hurry."

"You almost killed me!" he said.

"I said I was sorry," I said meekly.

"Well, you should be. Besides, girls shouldn't run like that."

"Says who?" I said. I squinched up my eyes at him.

"Everybody," he said.

"Who's everybody?" I said.

He shrugged. He took his hand away from his mouth and looked down at it, and his eyes grew wide and surprised looking. There was blood on his hand, and now that he had uncovered his face, I saw there was blood on his nose and on his mouth, too.

I had given him a bloody nose!

I reached in my pocket and took out my handkerchief. I untied Mamma's needles and my candies, then handed him the handkerchief, but I couldn't look at him.

I looked down at the ground, put a hand to my mouth, and bit my lip hard—but I couldn't help it. I giggled anyway.

"It's not funny!" he said.

"I know," I said. I took a deep breath and swallowed. But the laugh burst out of me.

"You bit me!" I said.

"I didn't bite you!" he said.

"Did, too," I said. I pushed my bonnet back so he could see the mark on my forehead.

"Well, it's your fault!" he said.

"Your fault, too," I said. "You should have yelled or something."

He made a face at me. "I did!"

I grinned at him. "Yell louder next time," I said.

He shook his head, glared at me, then wiped his face and mouth and nose. He shoved the handkerchief back at me, not even saying thank you.

I put it back in my pocket with the candies and packet of needles. "You're not very polite, are you?" I said.

"It wasn't very polite to run me over!" he said.

"Oh, stop being a baby," I said.

He glared at me, then wiped his hand on his pants. "Who are you?" he said.

"Abbie," I said. "Who are you?"

"By," he said.

"What?" I said.

"Byram. But everybody calls me By."

"Oh," I said. "Do you live in town?"

He nodded. "Sometimes. Lately I do. Where do you live?"

"On the prairie," I said, "along the river, about fifteen miles out."

"How'd you get here?" he said.

"On our wagon," I said.

"I can ride fifteen miles on my mule," he said. "Last week I went exploring for a whole day. I could find your place easy if it's on the river. Did you ever ride a mule?"

"I ride a horse sometimes," I said. "I wouldn't go fifteen miles on a mule, though. You'd get a sore rear end."

He shrugged. "Sometimes," he said, "but you get used to it. Maybe I'll come out and visit you tomorrow."

I looked at him, but I didn't believe him—not fifteen miles on a mule. Still, it would be nice to have a visitor.

"Do you know people in town?" I said.

"I know everybody in this town," he said. "I've been here just four weeks, and already I know everybody."

It was a braggy thing to say, but he didn't say it like he was bragging. He was simply matter-of-fact.

"Do you know Mr. Richardson's sisters?" I said.

His eyebrows went up. "Yeah," he said. "Why?"

"What are they like? I heard one of them is going to be the new schoolteacher."

He nodded. "Yup. She is."

"Do you know her?" I said.

Again he nodded. "Yup."

"Is she nice?" I said.

He grinned, and I noticed for the first time that he had a good face, with brown-red skin, almost as dark as an Indian, and he was kind of handsome—when he wasn't giving me that fierce look. There was a tiny gap between his front teeth, but his smile was nice, too.

"She's fair enough," he said. "You want to meet her?"

"Yes!" I said.

"Let's go," he said. "I'll take you."

He started leading me out of the alley. But then he stopped and turned back to me. "You want to fix yourself some first," he said.

I frowned at him. "Fix myself?"

He looked at my feet.

I looked down and saw what he meant. There were Nathaniel's trousers, peeking from beneath my skirts. I had put them on that morning, tied them with a rope around my waist, so I could ride bareback astride Maggie all the way home. The rope must have come loose when I was running, and now, there they were, hanging below my skirt.

"Don't look," I said.

He turned his back.

I reached under my skirt, pulled up the trousers, and tied the rope tighter. I straightened my skirt and smoothed it down.

"Turn around," I said.

He did.

"Do they still show?" I asked.

He looked at my feet and shook his head.

"All right," I said. "I'm ready. Let's go meet the teacher."

# Eight

NOBODY RUNS faster than me, not anyone I've ever met. But By came mighty close. We ran to the end of the alley, crossed the main street, dodging horses and ox teams, then turned and ran some more. We ran all the way to where the river meanders across the town's edge, before it gets more serious and runs on out to the prairie. By stopped and looked at me. I tried hard to breathe easy, to take long, slow breaths, to not let him know I was nearly panting. I was happy to see he was bending and resting his hands on his knees, a sure sign he was out of breath, too.

"See that?" he said. He pointed to a small island out in the middle of the river, so loaded with cottonwood trees that it seemed it might sink.

This time of year, the Platte River runs fast, even

though it's shallow. It rushed up to the island, then divided around it before rushing on again. It left bubbling places where it circled around the island, like it had forgotten to be a river and had become a spring.

"The island?" I said. "It's pretty. So's the river."

"No, the house!" he said.

I followed where he was pointing. And then I saw it, hidden almost under the cottonwoods. It was a small cabin, built right into the side of what looked like a beaver dam, the roof barely visible, with a stovepipe sticking out and a window in front.

"Somebody lives there?" I said.

By nodded. "Crazy Annie. She lives there year round, and just comes to town to get supplies. She's a witch, too. She does magic."

"Silly!" I said. "There's no such thing as magic."

"Is, too," By said. "I saw her doing it just last week, saw her with the sand cranes and whooping cranes. Ever see them?"

I nodded. "Lots of times," I said. "Mostly in the spring and the fall they come flying over the prairie. They're very, very big and very beautiful. And they're not magic."

"Annie made them dance!" he said.

I made a face at him.

"She did!" he said. "I was here one morning last week, and I watched. The whooping cranes were over there on the island. They were dancing in a circle, 'round and 'round, while Annie stood watching, nodding her head, like she was keeping time to music. She was making them dance faster and faster and faster!"

I rolled my eyes.

"Don't believe me," he said. "But they were. And something else—Annie puts a hex on people she doesn't like. Last week, she got mad at the blacksmith for the way he was shoeing a horse, and that night, there was a big storm and his whole place burned down, right to the ground."

I put my hands on my hips. "Probably hit by lightning," I said. "What's magic about that?"

He shrugged. "Don't believe me," he said. "But it's true. She had cholera. It made her crazy."

"So?" I said. "Lots of people get cholera. My papa's whole family died of cholera—all but his brother and he's not crazy. Cholera doesn't make you crazy."

He shrugged. "Maybe Annie had it worse than other people."

"I don't believe in witches," I said. "Besides, I heard that sand cranes and whooping cranes do a mating dance sometimes. That's probably what you saw. Anyway, forget Annie. Let's go meet the teacher."

By looked over at the island once more, and I looked, too. But no one was out—no Annie, no nobody.

"She's a witch," By said. "I'm sure of it. And crazy, too." And he started again along the path that bordered the river, taking us to the very edge of town.

The path was so narrow that we had to walk single file. I made a face at By's back. He reminded me of Nathaniel a little, always having to have the last word, to be the smartest. But I didn't want to argue with him, either, at least not until he had taken me to the teacher.

"So what's the teacher like?" I said, talking to his back.

"She's nice," he answered.

"When did you meet her?" I said.

He laughed. "A long time ago."

"My papa said she's only been in town a few weeks," I said.

"I know," By said.

The path ended then, becoming a small street, hardly wider than a lane. There was a row of houses facing the street, their backs along the river. Each house was set up right close to the next one, and they were small, maybe only two rooms. But it was a nice, clean street, and there were flowers in some of the yards. There was a mule tethered to a post in the yard of one house, and in another front yard, two little girls were playing hoops.

A small wooden sidewalk ran in front of the houses, just a few planks fastened together. We were able to walk on it side by side, and when I looked over at By, I could see he was smiling.

"What?" I said.

"What what?" he said.

I stopped short, squinching up my eyes at him. "What are you up to?" I said.

"Just taking you to the teacher," he said, looking back at me innocent-like.

"Where does she live?" I said.

"There!" he said, pointing to the house where the mule was. "It's the third house." He grinned at me again.

"So why are you grinning like that?" I said.

"I'm just smiling!" he said. "That's all! Can't I even smile if I feel like it?"

And then we were turning in at the third house and going up the walk. By wiped his feet a few times, then opened the door—without knocking!

"By!" I said.

But he was already across the doorsill, holding the door for me. I shook my head. I was not going into a stranger's house without being invited. I was backing up, when I heard a woman's voice.

"That you, By?"

"It's me, Mamma!" he said. "I brought someone to meet you."

By motioned me in, an even wider grin spreading over his face.

*Mamma?* He had called her *Mamma?* The teacher was his mamma? I felt my face grow hot. Why hadn't he told me?

"Will you come in!" By said impatiently. "You said you wanted to meet her."

It was dark inside, the walls made of dark, rough wood, but one long slant of sunlight was falling across a table under a window. A woman sat there, a partly darned sock in one hand, a basket of mending on the table before her. She wore a checked apron over her dress, and she had a mass of red hair that was swept up on top of her head, escaping in little tendrils down the sides. Her skin was white and smooth, and she was young—much too young to be a mamma! She was smiling at me, the friendliest kind of smile.

"Mamma," By said, "this is Abbie. She lives on the prairie, but she's in town today. She wanted to meet the new teacher." He looked at me then. "This is my mamma," he said.

"I'm Miss Richardson," the woman said, and she stood up, holding out a hand to me. "And aren't you a beautiful child!" she added.

I took her hand, feeling more flustered than I ever had in my life. All I could manage to say was "Hello," and even that came out croaky, like I was a big old frog.

I was meeting the teacher! I was actually holding her hand. And she said I was beautiful!

"Are you one of the children I'm going to teach?" she asked.

I nodded. "Yes," I said, my voice barely above a whisper. "There's me and my sister, Sarah, and my brother Nathaniel."

"How delightful," she said, letting go my hand and clasping hers together, just like Sarah does sometimes when she's happy. "We'll have a wonderful time in our school. I've heard I may have as many as twelve children."

I nodded. And then I blurted out a question, the way I know I'm not supposed to. "Are you really going to homestead?" I asked. "All by yourself on the prairie, without a husband? I mean, I heard about your sister, but are you really . . ."

She raised her eyebrows in surprise, and I closed my mouth, feeling the heat flooding my face again.

"Well," she said. "I see there are no secrets in this town."

"I didn't mean to pry," I said. "I mean, I just wondered." I thought of what Mamma would say—that I didn't think before I acted and spoke.

"Well, yes, we are going to homestead," Miss Richardson said. "My brother has picked out our tracts of land. And my sister, Emily, and I intend to homestead by ourselves—with the help of By, here." She turned and smiled at him.

It was mean of By, not letting me know about his mamma. But I really wasn't too mad; I was so glad to be here, to meet our new teacher! Wait till I told Sarah and Nathaniel!

And then I thought—how could she be *Miss* Richardson if she was By's mamma? Unless she had adopted him, like the people Papa told me about. By was dark skinned, almost Indian looking, so he could be adopted. But I knew I was definitely not supposed to ask about adopting.

"Can you read, Abbie?" Miss Richardson asked.

I nodded. "Oh, yes," I said. "We had a teacher last year. Well, sort of a teacher. And my papa has been reading us stories since I was very little."

"That's wonderful," she said. "A smart girl. Have you ever done a recitation?"

"Lots of times!" I told her. "Back in St. Joseph."

"That's good," she said.

"Are we going to have recitations?" I asked.

She smiled. "Perhaps."

"I like recitations," I said. "My sister does, too. But Nathaniel doesn't."

And then I heard the noon church bells ringing. "It's noon!" I said. "I have to go. I'm supposed to meet Papa at the wagon at noon."

"Do you know your way around?" Miss Richardson said. "Or should By go with you?"

I shook my head. I knew if I followed the river path I'd be back in the center of town in no time. "It's all right," I said. "I know the way."

"Good-bye, then," Miss Richardson said, and she took my hand again. "I'm so glad to have met you, Abbie. Tell your parents and brother and sister I'm looking forward to meeting them, too. We hope to be out in about a month, and we'll come calling on your mamma then."

"I'll come calling tomorrow!" By said. "Maybe."

I waved and hurried out and along the path back to town, my mind tumbling with thoughts. I had met the teacher and she was nice, really, really nice. She had said I was beautiful, that I was smart! And By would be our neighbor. He was a boy, but he wasn't too bad. A boy and a teacher and new neighbors, and it was all going to happen soon.

Child soon.

# Nine

I MET Papa at the wagon, and we ate our dinner sitting on a bench in front of the courthouse. While we ate, I told him everything—how I had met Miss Richardson, the teacher, how I'd met By, that they were coming soon to their homestead. I even told him about Crazy Annie. Papa listened and smiled in that slow, gentle way he has. When I was all finished, he said, "I haven't seen you this excited since we came out here."

"I haven't been this excited, Papa!" I said. "Just think—a real teacher. And other children. She said maybe twelve children. Where would they come from?"

"I'm not sure," Papa said. "It depends on where we set up the schoolhouse. It still has to be worked out."

"What kind of schoolhouse will we have?" I said. "A real one? I mean, like in St. Joseph?"

Papa shrugged. "Depends on if we can get wood."

"There's wood for these buildings," I said, looking around. "So why couldn't we get wood for a school?"

"Money," Papa said. "It costs a lot to haul in lumber. And there aren't many trees to cut down here."

I sighed. "It's always money!"

Papa laughed. "You've already learned a fact of life," he said.

"Well," I said, "there must be a way to get the money." I screwed up my face, thinking. "There's the school tax to pay the teacher," I said. "So why don't they use some of that money to—"

"Don't try to figure it all out, Abbie," Papa said. "That's what grown-ups are for."

"But sometimes grown-ups don't figure it out," I said.

Papa laughed again.

I looked across the street, thinking about all these big buildings and how I wanted a real school. That's when I saw the land office and the sign in the window. AUCTION! LAND SALE! it said. JULY THIRD AND FOURTH, FESTIVAL DAYS.

Suddenly, I could feel my heart thumping hard in my throat. "Papa?" I said, pointing across the street. "Do you see that? Does that mean us?"

Papa nodded.

"You mean we have to buy out this time?" I said. "Next month? Fourth of July?"

Papa nodded. "Yes," he said. "That's right."

"But, Papa?" I said. "It's so soon!"

"It is," he said. "But we've already had the twelve months allotted to prove out. They gave us an extension this spring, so now it's our time."

I took a big breath, but I held back the words I was thinking: Do we have the money? Do we, Papa?

For a while, neither of us spoke, and Papa began gathering our dinner things. "I think you'd better be getting on home," he said.

When I didn't answer, Papa put a finger under my chin, lifting my face. "Don't you worry, girl," he said. "Money is my worry."

"But, Papa," I said, "I do worry. July Fourth weekend is only a month away!"

"A lot can happen in a month," Papa said, smiling. "Look at what God created in just six days! Don't worry," he said. "All we need is a month of good weather so I can work full-time. That should give us about enough money to put us over the top. It's all I can do—work and pray. But we can't trouble our heads over it."

"Well, my head is troubled," I said. "What if we don't have the money?"

Papa stood up and reached for my hand. "Then we'll have to do something else," he said softly.

Like what? I wanted to say. But I didn't.

Instead, I let Papa take my hand, and we walked over to the wagon. The questions were tumbling around inside my head: Would we move back to town if he didn't have the money? Which town? This one or back to Missouri? Or would Papa just move us farther on across the prairie, and we'd have to start all over again? Or . . .

I climbed up into the wagon, and Papa walked along beside, holding the reins, leading Maggie, staying with me till we were at the edge of town.

At the place where the town petered out and the prairie began, Papa handed me Maggie's reins. "Go safely!" he said. "I'll be home when I can. Be good to your mamma and sister and brothers."

"I will, Papa," I said.

"I know you will," Papa said. "You're a good girl, Abbie." He smiled at me. "And try not to worry your head."

I took a deep breath. "I'll try," I said.

"Then all is well," Papa said. And he patted Maggie on the rump and sent us heading off home, back across the prairie.

We rode for a mile or so, but I kept feeling that Maggie's hooves were clumping out one sound, one word—*money*. What if Papa couldn't come up with the money? What would happen to us? To him?

After a while, though, I stopped thinking about money and began thinking about all the good things that were happening—like Miss Richardson and the school, about how excited Sarah and Nathaniel would be when I told them. How excited Mamma would be when I told her she'd have neighbors soon.

Something else. I did have Nathaniel's trousers on. And I did have the prairie all to myself.

I smiled, then slowed Maggie to a halt. Then I

tucked my skirt down into the trousers and climbed up on Maggie's back. Managing the harness was a bit tricky, but I did it, and we started up again, me astride Maggie, the wagon trailing along behind.

There were so many things to see on the prairie, and being up on Maggie's back made it even better. Now, I could see a whole herd of buffalo far off, moving slow and easy across the plains. I could see wildflowers everywhere. Prairie chickens scooted about, looking so much like the earth that I only saw them when I was almost on top of them. I saw a herd of antelope, shy and skittish, bouncing along like they were on springs.

I could hear the wind whispering in the grasses, hear the birds twittering, calling to one another. I tried to recognize each bird from its call, the way Papa had taught me. I recognized a dove's mournful *coo, coo,* and I heard the sound of some wood finches. Under me, I could feel the earth shift as the buffalo moved far out over the prairie.

After a while, I began to feel awfully hot, and I looked for a place to give Maggie a rest and some shade. There are almost no trees on the prairie, but every little while, a small part of the Platte River breaks out of its banks and meanders a ways onto the prairie, and when it does, a line of cottonwoods grow, just like they do behind our soddy.

Now, I spotted a grove and headed for it. I climbed down and let Maggie loose. I tethered her to a stake I carried in the wagon so she could drink from the stream and rest awhile. Then I lay down under a tree to rest, too. I could hear the scurrying of some prairie hens, the scuttle of a small animal near the bank of the river. I saw something dark—an otter? a beaver?—hurrying down the bank between the tree roots, then diving and disappearing into the water.

I rolled over onto my stomach and watched where it had gone, leaving a ripple like a path, a sign that said: this is where I am.

Maggie didn't bother to look. She just continued to drink, the skin on her sides twitching, her tail switching, too, as she shooed off flies.

I turned onto my back and closed my eyes—and then opened them again, because suddenly I felt I was being watched.

My heart sped up, and all I could think of was Indians. They wanted me, wanted my scalp.

I looked around. No Indians.

And then I saw what was watching me. A female antelope was standing by the end of the wagon, seeming to peer out from behind it. She was so close I could almost feel her warm breath, and she was looking at me, her eyes wide, liquid, not at all afraid. She moved forward a little, her delicate hooves making a clacking sound where she stepped on a tree root. She tilted her head sideways, ears cocked forward, like she was about to speak to me.

"Hello," I said softly.

At that, she turned and fled, practically flying, bounding away from me just like the ones I had seen earlier.

I wondered what she thought as she ran away. Did she think anything? Do animals think?

I'd asked Mamma that once. We had taken Maggie out to gather buffalo chips, and when we had finished and were close to home, Maggie began to speed up. I told Mamma it was because Maggie was imagining her day was done, was picturing herself bedded down with some hay and a bucket of oats.

But Mamma said it was pure instinct that made Maggie hustle, that Maggie didn't have a thought in her head. I was pretty sure Mamma was wrong about that. That antelope was thinking something, and she would tell the other antelopes when she caught up with them.

I thought of Mamma then, how she would scold me for my fanciful thoughts, and I said my now-familiar prayer—that I would be sensible, content, that I would please Mamma more.

It was all so peaceful here, so quiet, that I closed my eyes to rest a bit. And then I slept.

# Ten

WHEN I woke, I could see the shadows long and blue, and the sun low in the sky. The wind had died down, the way it always does on the prairie in the evening, and the birds were beginning to twitter and talk. When we lived in St. Joseph, I always thought birds just twittered when they woke up. But at night on the prairie, the birds get chatty just before it's time to sleep—maybe having to say all the things they didn't get said in the daytime. I smiled. Sometimes Sarah and I were like that, too, talking quietly in bed before we fell asleep.

I looked at the sky, at the sun low now, and thought I'd better get moving. Mamma might be worried.

I hitched Maggie up again. I pulled out the stake

I'd tied her to and threw it into the wagon. Mamma would be pleased at that, since I'd lost more than one stake, forgetting it in the grass. I took off Nathaniel's trousers, buried them under the straw, and straightened my skirt around me. That done, we started off.

I was still a mile or so from home, when I saw a girl all alone, walking out on the prairie, her skirts blowing around her. Sarah? I was too far off to tell for sure, but who else? Then I got nearer, and it was Sarah. But a mile from home?

I clucked at Maggie, making her speed up. "Come on, girl," I said.

I smiled, thinking how Sarah must be missing me today, with no one to talk to. But it was odd that Mamma had let her come so far alone. And Sarah hardly ever does what Mamma says not to do.

I stood up in the wagon and yelled, "Yoo-hoo! Sarah! We're coming."

She lifted a hand and waved back, and then she started running.

When she was alongside, I leaned down from the wagon seat and gave her my hand. She sprang up into the seat beside me, as if she were no heavier than a dove feather.

"Where have you been?" she cried.

"Where have I been?" I said. "In town, you know that."

"But what took you so long? Mamma has been worried sick."

"It's not that late," I said, looking around. The

sun was still up, although low in the sky. "Well, only a little late."

"It's very late! And besides . . ."

"Besides, I'm a girl!" I said. "Nathaniel stays and Mamma doesn't worry. He hardly ever comes home till supper time."

"Nathaniel's a boy," she said. "Mamma worries different about you. And you've even missed supper. Besides . . ."

"Besides, it's dumb," I said.

"Abbie?" Sarah said. "You're not listening. Nathaniel's sick. And Charlie is, too."

"Charlie, too?" I said.

"Very sick," Sarah said. "Mamma is worried half frantic."

Mamma, frantic? That was hard to picture, hard to believe. She is calm in crises, much calmer than Papa.

"She's been waiting for you. We need you to go for the doctor," Sarah said.

"Now?" I said. "Almost night?"

Sarah didn't say anything. And I felt this heavy place suddenly, this ache in my middle, weighing me down. I'd been dumb again, addle-brained. Mamma needed me at home, she'd needed me a lot earlier, and I'd been daydreaming about antelope. I'd been sleeping!

"Come on, Maggie," I said, and I stood and shook the reins, bringing her to a trot.

We were almost home, so Maggie was speeding up anyway, thinking of her oats.

When we pulled up in front of the soddy, no one

was about—just the chickens pecking in the dirt and the wind waving a flag Papa had put up over the well.

"Mamma?" I called.

I handed the reins to Sarah. "Hold this and be ready to go out again," I said.

I jumped down from the wagon as Mamma came to the door of the soddy.

Her face was flushed, her eyes hard. The lines down her cheeks were deeper than I'd ever seen before, like she had grown older in only one day.

"Mamma?" I said. "Do you need me to go for the doctor?"

Mamma nodded, her eyes still with that cold, hard look.

"Mamma?" I said.

She didn't answer, just kept looking at me.

I jumped back up into the wagon, as Sarah jumped down.

"No!" Mamma said, reaching for Sarah and pushing her back toward the wagon. "Go with Abbie. No telling where she'll go to if you don't keep an eye on her."

I felt this ache, like Mamma had hit me, felt the tears spring to my eyes.

"Mamma?" I said. "Mamma, I'm sorry. I just didn't think—"

"That's your trouble!" Mamma said. She looked away from me and out to the prairie, like she couldn't bear to see me. "That's your trouble!" she said again. "You never think!"

I looked down and gathered up the reins. And then I did think.

"Hold these," I said to Sarah, and I handed her the reins.

Then I ran around to the shed, got some feed and oats for Maggie, and some water, too.

When I came back, Mamma had disappeared inside the soddy. After a minute, she reappeared and handed Sarah something wrapped in a cloth, bread probably, and a water jug. She also handed up the lantern and some matches in a tin. "You'll need these. It'll be dark soon," she said. "Because, Lord knows, I can't lose two sons and two daughters in the same day."

"Lose them!" I said. "Mamma, nobody's dying. Are they?"

Mamma didn't answer.

"Mamma?" I said.

"Get on with you!" Mamma said.

"We're going, Mamma," I said. "And we'll be all right, I promise. We'll go directly there and directly back."

"That you will," Mamma said. She turned and disappeared into the soddy.

Sarah and I started back to town again, neither of us speaking. I didn't know what Sarah was thinking, but I was remembering the day in town, playing and teasing and running, meeting By and pretending to see witches, listening to antelope thoughts, admiring myself in shop windows. And all that time, Charlie was sick, and Nathaniel, too, and I should have come home directly, but no, I had to play and ride bareback and fall asleep and now . . .

Now, Maggie's hooves were silent, didn't say anything, didn't sigh about money, didn't sing about antelope. They said nothing, nothing at all but *clop-clop, clop-clop.*

But if they had, I knew what they would have said, and I felt the tears come to my eyes again. That's your trouble, they would say, you never think. Never think. Never, never, never think.

# Eleven

Doc Svenson was new in town. He had come to take the place of old Dr. Thor, who had been killed falling off a wagon. Doc Svenson hadn't yet been to our place, so we'd have to show him the way.

When we got to his house and told him about Charlie and Nathaniel, he went right away to hitch up his fancy horse and buggy. Watching him, I had a thought—his horse was much faster than our old plodding Maggie. Maybe Sarah could ride with him and show him the way. They'd get there faster, and I could come on behind.

Sarah nodded when I told her this. Her little face was pinched and worried looking, and she'd hardly said a word in the wagon, only asking once if we should try and find Papa. I wanted to so much. He'd help, Papa would. But I said no. I knew it would take a while, and Mamma had been so upset. Doc Svenson said he thought having Sarah ride with him was a mighty fine suggestion. "Good thinking!" he said, smiling at me. "You're a right smart girl."

I shrugged. The first smart thought I'd had all day.

So Sarah and Doc Svenson took off together, and I turned old Maggie around and we followed.

We were a short ways onto the plains when I lost sight of Doc Svenson's carriage completely and could see only the dust rising behind them.

The sun was gone by then, down below the rim of the earth, although there was still enough rosy light left to see by. Still, I knew the way—and Maggie surely knew it, could feel the path through the grasses, the way the river meandered back and forth, could see, even in the dark, the line of cottonwoods.

We went very slowly homeward. I knew Maggie must be tired, and I allowed her to take her time, even though it sometimes seemed she was falling asleep right in her traces. She plodded slowly, her head down, seeming not only tired but maybe sad, too.

Fanciful thoughts. Like a horse could feel sad. Like an antelope could think.

Like Mamma was talking inside my head.

I broke off some of the bread Mamma had sent along, ate it, and drank some water. The candy was still in my pocket, but I didn't want it now. I would save it for when the boys got better.

I tried not to think about what was happening back at the soddy. Was Nathaniel terribly sick? Charlie, too? Were they dying? No! Not dying.

Sing, that's what I could do. I could sing to myself, just like Papa always tells us, make a joyful noise and chase away bad thoughts. But when I began a lullaby, my voice sounded so lonely, the only sound on the prairie, that I quickly shut my mouth again.

I looked up at the big blue-black sky and saw the first star hanging there, the evening star.

Papa always says we should wish on the evening star.

I wished hard—that Charlie and Nathaniel would get better, that Mamma wouldn't be angry with me.

I looked ahead, and suddenly, way out on the horizon, I saw a long line of something moving—wolves or coyotes, coming on single file, the way the Indians sometimes did, silhouetted against the sky.

I watched them creep along, my heart beating faster. If they were hungry and smelled us, they might come after us. I pictured the way they'd circle around, leaping at Maggie's throat, darting between her legs, pushing her off balance until they got her down, and one of them would strike, tearing her throat open. I'd seen them do it to a cow once.

I looked around me. I had no rifle. But I could make lots of noise to scare them if they came, maybe use the stake to pound against the sides of the wagon. After a few moments, though, they headed off somewhere else, seeming not to know we were there.

Still, I clucked at Maggie, urging her on a little

faster, anxious to be home. I wondered what Mamma would think when she saw the doctor's carriage pull up without me following. Would she be angry, thinking I was dawdling again? But Sarah would set her straight. Maybe Doc Svenson would tell Mamma what he had told me—I was a good thinker.

Dark was fully down upon me by the time I pulled up to the soddy. I could see the lamp inside, see the doctor's horse and buggy tied up to the fence.

"I'm home!" I shouted, and heard Mamma shout back. I unhitched Maggie, led her to her shed, and gave her plenty of oats and water. I rubbed her down, soothed her, and told her what a good, good horse she was.

Finally, she was fed and settled, and I took Nathaniel's trousers from the wagon and hung them on the back line. Then I went 'round front to the soddy, almost tripping in the dark over a mattress by the door. A mattress? Why? Had Mamma pulled it out for the boys earlier, when it was too hot inside?

I stood outside the door for a moment, listening, but there was hardly any sound, just the murmuring of a voice and what sounded like Nathaniel moaning. Odd that the door was closed when I knew it would be so hot inside. I had my hand on the door, when it suddenly opened from within, and Sarah came out, holding our quilt and pillow and Emmaline.

"You can't go in," she said, pulling the door closed behind her. "We're to sleep out here."

"Outside?" I said. "Why?"

"Doc Svenson said he'd stay the night. And he doesn't want us in there."

"Why not?" I said.

"Here, help me," she said. She bent, and I helped her spread the quilt on top of the mattress.

Sarah straightened up and looked at me, her eyes dark and wide and scared. "Doc Svenson's afraid we'll catch the sickness from the boys," she said.

"What sickness?" I asked.

Sarah shivered, hugging her arms to herself. "He thinks they have cholera," she whispered.

I sucked in my breath, remembering about Papa's papa and his wife, who had died of cholera. They were fine in the morning and were dead by nightfall.

"Cholera?" I said.

"That's what he said," she answered.

"Maybe he's wrong," I said. "Maybe it's something else. Maybe it's just colic or something."

Sarah didn't answer.

"Sarah?" I said. "Are they going to . . . Did he say they'd be all right?"

"No!" Sarah said. "He said he didn't know. And I'm scared."

She turned to me, and I quickly went to her and wrapped my arms around her, holding her close.

"I'm scared," she whispered.

"I'm scared, too," I whispered back.

Her little body trembled in my arms, and I thought how tiny she was, how frail. We stood holding on to each other for a while, and then she pulled away. We both lay down on the mattress, and I covered us with the quilt.

Sarah hugged Emmaline to her, and I suddenly wished that I had a doll to hold, too. I'd never been so scared. Indians on horseback, a single file of wolves on the prairie, Crazy Annie who might be a witch. None of that was scary. This was scary.

For a long time I lay staring up at the sky, at the blanket of stars glittering white above me, seeming to pulse with light, the long wash of white that was the Milky Way. I lay there and I prayed. Dear God, I prayed, God who made the sky and the stars, who made antelope and buffalo and the prairie, who made me and Sarah and Nathaniel and Charlie, dear God. I won't ever ask for anything again, just answer this prayer. I don't care about a piano or about living in town, and this old soddy is fine. I don't even mind the dirt that falls from the roof into our dinner or even the bugs. And, dear God, I'll do anything, anything at all. I'll even give you all the money in my wishing bag, everything in the world. I'll stop daydreaming, I'll stop imagining, and I won't dawdle, and I won't be addle-brained, and I won't ever wear Nathaniel's trousers again or ride astride and bareback, I promise. I'll be satisfied with my lot, and please, God, please, just this once, answer this prayer: Make my brothers better. Amen.

# Twelve

IT WAS still dark, with just a faint line of light showing in the eastern sky, when something awakened me. My head was aching something fierce, and there was a gnawing in my stomach. I heard an owl hoot in the cottonwoods, heard another one answer, and I lay listening, feeling the emptiness in my stomach and wondering why I hadn't eaten before bed. And why was I sleeping out of doors?

And then it all came back. I sat up, feeling my head swim when I moved, and looked around me.

Mamma was standing at the door of the soddy, the lamplight shining behind her.

In her arms was Charlie—Charlie sleeping, not crying. Charlie!

I scrambled to my feet, being careful not to disturb Sarah, and hurried to Mamma, feeling weak and dizzy.

"Mamma!" I whispered, bending close to look down at Charlie's sleeping face. "How is he, Mamma? Is he all right now?"

"Yes," Mamma said, her voice mournful, low. "He's all right now. He's with God."

"Mamma!" I cried.

"Hush," she said. "Hush now. It's God's will. Charlie's all right now. It's for the best."

"No, Mamma!" I said. "No!"

"Hush," she said again. She hugged Charlie to her then, hugged him close, began rocking herself and him, cradling him crosswise to her chest. Holding him like that, she looked like she was nursing him, and I felt tears running down my face, choking my throat.

"Mamma!" I said.

For a long time, Mamma just stood there, hugging Charlie, rocking him. And then, slowly, she lifted her head.

"Abbie!" she said. She held out both arms, held Charlie out to me, his little round face smooth and peaceful, his eyelids closed. He was just sleeping. Dreaming.

"Here," Mamma said softly. "Hold your brother. Say good-bye."

"Mamma!" I said. "No!"

I backed up, looked at Mamma, at Charlie dead in her arms.

I shook my head again.

And then I had this awful thought—Nathaniel!

"Mamma!" I said. "Mamma—Nathaniel?"

"Doc Svenson thinks he'll be all right," Mamma said.

And then Sarah was standing beside us, holding on to my skirt, the way she used to when she was very little.

"Mamma?" she whispered. "Is it true?"

"Yes, it's true," Mamma said. "Charlie's gone to God, and that's the truth."

I turned away, snatching my skirt loose from Sarah's hand, and walked away from them.

I walked across the yard to the fence and stood holding tight to it, feeling the earth seeming to swirl around me, my head aching, stomach hurting. The sky was getting lighter, and the birds were waking up, crows barking from the treetops, the rooster announcing it was morning. Even Heather, our cow, was lowing softly somewhere back of the stream, asking to be milked; the whole stupid prairie was coming awake. Only Charlie wouldn't wake up.

Behind me, I heard Mamma's voice, that low tone I'd never heard before, mournful like the wind.

"Doc Svenson is young," Mamma said. "He has newfangled ideas. He thinks we should bury Charlie right away. He thinks we shouldn't touch him, shouldn't say good-bye to him. He says we'll get sick from holding him. Imagine, such foolishness!"

There was a pause, but Sarah didn't answer, or if she did, her voice was too soft to hear. In a moment,

Mamma spoke again, her voice ringing clear in the morning air.

"We'll get sick from not touching him," Mamma said. "And that's the truth."

I turned around from the fence and looked at Mamma, at Sarah holding Mamma's skirt, at Charlie dead in Mamma's arms, Mamma cradling Charlie to her, rocking him, rocking him.

Charlie was dead. And it had taken me too long to get the doctor.

Mamma looked over at me. "Come, Abbie," she said. "We have work to do. The cow has to be milked and Nathaniel's still too sick to do it. Dr. Svenson will tell Papa about Charlie when he goes back to town. We have to wash Charlie, get him ready for burial, dress him."

I didn't answer, just looked at her.

"Come," Mamma said again. "We need your help now."

I still couldn't answer, but I started back to her, feeling the earth seem to move and heave beneath me.

Mamma started toward me and met me halfway across the yard. She leaned close to me, so close that I could feel Charlie's little body pressed between us. "You needn't hold him, my dear," Mamma said to me softly, the first time she had ever called me that. "But do say good-bye."

And then, an aching, fierce rage welled up and I turned away.

"No!" I said. I said it very softly, inside me, no

sound coming out. “No!” I said again, out loud this time. “I'm going to milk Heather.”

I turned and headed for the back, half stumbling from the pain in my head, and got the bucket from the shed. All the way, the tears fell down and watered my face and my skirt and fell on my hands and into my ears, but what could I do?

I scrambled down the little hillock, but Heather was gone. Again, she was gone! Dumb cow! I could hear the tinkle of her bell, hear her lowing from across the stream. I put a hand to my head. I was hot, all hot, and sad, and my stomach and head ached, and is this how it felt when someone died? I waded across the stream, holding up my skirt, steadying myself by grabbing onto tree roots, and scrambled up the little ravine. Dumb cow, she got off her tether too much. But no matter, Charlie didn't need her milk now.

I started up the ravine, and I suddenly felt a need for the outhouse. I needed it bad, but I was too far away, so I just squatted on the earth, and then I was sick. I was so sick.

I rested a moment, then straightened myself the best I could and started out again, looking for Heather. My head was aching, my eyes were aching, and I felt hot and mixed up in my head.

I could hear Papa's words, Papa's voice, saying all is well, all is well, and talking about the land, the land sale, land for my sons, yes, for my sons. But Charlie didn't need land now, and, besides, he wouldn't be dead if we lived in town, if we hadn't moved out to the prairie, people didn't get sick to death in towns, or if they did, the doctor would come, he'd come fast. It wouldn't take him forever like it did last night.

I laid my head against the trunk of a tree and let the tears run.

And then, when the tears were all used up, I went on, up the little ravine, out along the stream, through the cottonwoods, stumbling, half falling, my head aching, listening, looking for the cow, listening for her bell. Because, like Mamma said, there was work to do.

# Thirteen

I DON'T remember much after that. I remember only the sharp sound of hooves, the sound a mule makes—or maybe it was the antelope. I remember arms lifting me up, but antelopes don't have arms. And then I was slung on the back of a mule—or was it an antelope?—and someone was taking me somewhere, home. Home. To St. Joseph, back in Missouri. Except it seemed different, so maybe it wasn't St. Joseph at all.

It was hot where they took me, that I remember; my head was burning up, and Mamma was doing something to my head, cool and wet, something cool, and then Papa was doing it, too; and I wanted to see Sarah, but she wouldn't come to me, they wouldn't let her in the soddy—or was it the house? I heard her, though, heard her outside, and she was talking, and it sounded like By she was talking to, but of course it wasn't By; he was in town. And Nathaniel was all better—I knew he was because I could hear him reading to me, beside my bed. And Papa was home, so there was no work in the town, or we were in St. Joseph or maybe in Grand Island, and Papa came home some nights, even came for dinner at noon. He read to me, too, and I heard those fancy, pretty words—*Ptolemais, Agabus*—and then he read from Romans: " 'If we have died with Christ, having risen we shall die no more, for death shall have no dominion over us. . . .' "

I was tired and knew something bad had happened, but each time I started to remember, it slid away again, and I closed my eyes tighter to keep it away.

I heard voices, lots of voices, someone strange—that new doctor, the one who said I was good at thinking, a smart young lady. But I wasn't. I was too dumb, too bad.

And then I started to remember again. But I couldn't wake up—couldn't, wouldn't think.

For a long time I stayed like that. But then, one morning—I know it was morning because the sky was pink through the open door—I woke up and knew I was awake.

I must have made a sound, because Papa was bending over me, looking down at me.

"Oh, come quick!" I heard him say. "Come quick."

And then Mamma was standing over me, too, in her white nightdress, her hair in one long braid over her shoulder.

"You're awake!" Papa said. And he was crying, tears in his voice, tears down his face.

And then I remembered. Charlie was dead. Papa was crying for Charlie.

That's when I began to cry.

I closed my eyes and turned away from him.

I felt Papa sit on the mattress. He put a hand on my cheek. "Don't cry," he said. "Don't cry. You're better now. There's nothing to cry about."

"I'll get the water on," Mamma said. She touched me—I know it was her touch on the top of my head—and I heard her say, "Thank God."

I still didn't want to think. We were in this rotten soddy, and it was hot. And I wanted to go home. I wanted to go to St. Joseph, to go home.

I opened my eyes and looked around. My eyes ached, burned and ached, and I was tired. Where was Sarah? Nathaniel?

Charlie?

Charlie was dead. I looked over at the fireplace. His little cradle was gone.

Papa was looking down at me, his face full of—what? Wonder, it looked like, surprise. "Dear girl," he said. Over and over he said it. "Dear girl, dear, dear girl."

"Papa?" I said. "Papa, what . . ." I started to say, what happened? But I couldn't. I knew what had happened. Charlie was dead. My baby brother was dead.

Instead I said, "Where's Sarah? Nathaniel?"

Papa put a hand on my forehead, smoothing back

my hair. "Outside," he said. "They've been sleeping outside. It's much cooler out there. But they've been here, by your side. Every single day they've been talking to you, reading to you. Even when you were unconscious, they read to you." He leaned close to me, then, and put his face right against mine. "They've saved your candy for you, too," he said. "Wouldn't even eat theirs till you were all better."

"But, Papa," I said. "What happened? Why am I here? Why am I in bed?"

"Oh, my dear," Papa said. "You've been sick. Very, very sick. For almost two weeks now you've been sick and we've prayed over you and watched over you. You collapsed out on the plains, and the good Lord must have been watching over you, too, because someone found you and carried you home."

"I know," I said, "the antelope."

Papa stroked my forehead, smiling at me. "No," he said, "not an antelope. Your friend, By. You met him in town that day, remember? He came out on his mule that day you fell sick and was looking for this place. He found you by the stream, far away. You'd have died if he'd not found you."

"Oh," I said.

And then I thought: Maybe I should have died. Because I'm so bad, such a bad person. But how could I say that?

Again, I began to cry.

Papa leaned over me, his head right on the pillow. "Tell me," he said. "Say whatever it is."

I wanted to tell him, Lord, I wanted to. It was

ready to burst out of me. But how could I when he'd hate me, too, just the way Mamma must hate me? My fault.

I couldn't, so instead, I took a big, shaky breath. "I'm just sad," I said. "That's all."

"I know," Papa said. "We're all sad. But things will be better. You've had cholera, but you're better now, and you're going to get stronger and stronger till you're all well."

"But, Papa?" I said. "Charlie won't get better. Charlie's dead. Where did you put his cradle, Papa?"

"Yes," Papa said, and I saw him blink. His face got scrunched up, and I saw the tears start again.

"Yes, my dear," Papa said, wiping his face with both hands, wiping away the tears. "Charlie is dead. He went to God."

"Why, Papa?" I said.

Papa just looked at me, and then he reached down and took my hand, and his was wet with his tears.

"Why, Papa?" I said. "Why would God want a baby?"

For a minute, Papa didn't answer. And then he said, "My dear, I don't know. I honestly, truly, don't know."

"Papa?" I said. "Papa, can I tell you something?"

"Yes," Papa said. "Anything."

"Well," I said. I took a deep breath. "Papa, I think God is dreadful," I said. "I think God is truly, truly dreadful."

I didn't know what Papa would say, if he'd get angry. He didn't look angry, but he didn't speak either, not for a very long time. He just kept stroking my hand. And then, he said, "Yes, my dear, there are times I get so weak and troubled, I feel that way, too."

For a long time after, I just lay staring up at the roof, at the bits of grass and weeds that were growing right out of the ceiling, with Papa holding my hand and stroking it. Sometimes I would look over at Papa, but he wasn't looking at me. He seemed to be seeing something inside his head.

I looked back at the ceiling then, at the fireplace where Charlie's cradle wasn't anymore, at the door and the sun blazing up over the horizon, orange, hot. I looked at Papa again.

"Papa?" I said. "Papa, can we go home now?"

Papa let go of my hand, stroked my forehead again. "You are home," he said softly. "Your friend, By, he found you and brought you home. Remember?"

"No," I said. "I didn't mean that. I meant home, really home to St. Joseph. Missouri. Can we go home now?"

Papa took a deep breath, slow and long, then let it out in a great sigh. And then he sighed again. "I'm thinking about it, Abbie," he said. "I've been thinking about it."

# Fourteen

THE DAYS had a strange feel to them after that. They felt very long and very short, all at the same time. It seemed all I did was sleep and wake up, sleep and wake up. Usually someone was beside me when I woke up—Sarah or Nathaniel or Mamma. Papa had gone back to town, but Mamma said he was going to walk out to us on Saturday night, or maybe Nathaniel would go get him in the wagon. I wondered what Papa was planning. Would we stay? Would we go? Did he have the land-sale money?

Sometimes I cared. Other times, I didn't care at all. But I knew I shouldn't say anything about it again.

When I wasn't sleeping, I tried walking, but I quickly found that I was so weak I could stand only for a minute. I had to go on hands and knees sometimes, just as if I was a baby, not even toddling like Charlie. As soon as I thought of Charlie, the tears started up again. Then I'd have to sit down till the tears were gone, 'cause it seemed I couldn't stand, or even crawl, and cry at the same time.

And that was another strange thing about those days—I was crying all the time. I don't think I was crying *for* anything—except those times I was crying for Charlie. I think I just had to cry. Maybe it came from being sick for such a long time. I finally understood why Sarah had gotten so quiet, so thoughtful last winter. Something about being sick made you quiet, made you think a lot. It made me think a lot, even though Mamma always says I never stop to think. I felt as though I had a lot to figure out. But what those things were, I had no idea.

Then one morning I woke up knowing I was a lot stronger. It was very early, the sun barely creeping above the horizon, and I stole out of bed, careful to be extra quiet and not disturb anyone.

Mamma opened her eyes instantly, though, and sat up.

"I'm all right," I whispered. "I need to use the outhouse."

"Use the chamber pot," Mamma said.

I shook my head. "I'm strong enough," I answered. "Really."

Mamma looked worried, her face pulled into that frown she has lately. She nodded, though, then lay back down, but she still watched me as I stepped over Nathaniel and Sarah on my way to the door.

At the doorway, I turned, looked back at her, and smiled.

Mamma nodded again.

I had hardly looked at Mamma since I'd gotten better. I didn't want to see what would be in her eyes.

I started walking to the outhouse, feeling strong enough, really better. My legs weren't trembling, and I didn't have to hold on to the fence or to tree roots.

I made it all the way to the outhouse, not having to drop to my hands and knees even once. Then I started back, looking around me, really seeing things for the first time since I'd been sick. Summer was on the prairie now, the garden rich with ripening corn and squash and tomatoes, all those things Mamma would try and put up by winter. The berry bushes were laden. Birds were singing and calling, and in the grass there were rustlings, as if everything was alive and even underground things were feeling the warmth of the sun.

The sky was the truly clear blue that it gets only in summer, and already, this early in the morning, the wind was beginning to blow. I think that's the first thing I ever noticed about the prairie, the way the wind blows and blows and blows. I love the wind, love the way you can count on it, the way it never seems to stop, except at night. Mamma doesn't like it. She says its constant blowing makes her nervy—about the only thing she ever complains about. I wondered if I would miss the wind if we moved back to St. Joseph.

Looking around, I suddenly thought of something. Where was Charlie buried? Practically every family that comes to the prairie has its own burial place. But we'd never needed to bury anyone—not since in St. Joseph when Grandfather died—and I wondered what place Papa or Mamma had chosen.

I climbed across tiny ravine and stood looking over the prairie.

Yes, there it was. I could barely see it, beyond the line of cottonwoods, a small cross on the rise in the midst of all the wildflowers. I knew then that Papa had chosen this place. He'd put Charlie where there were lots of flowers for him.

I walked to the small place that Papa had fenced off, then sat down to rest, leaning my head against the fence. It's so hard to get wood on the prairie, with just the few cottonwoods that grow along the stream, that I wondered how Papa had been able to find enough to make such a strong-looking enclosure. I knew you needed one—it kept the wolves out—and thinking that made me cry again.

I just sat there looking at the little cross, and let myself cry for a long time; I don't know how long. I do know that the sun came up, and then I began to feel a little better.

I stood up, wiped my eyes, and scanned the prairie. And that's when I saw something moving, something small, a tiny black dot moving—toward us? Away?

I stood on tiptoe, shading my eyes with my hand.

It was coming toward us, whatever it was, something small, a person? Someone on a horse? It wasn't big enough to be a wagon, but it was surely moving. And probably not an Indian, because they never came singly.

I started back down the ravine to the soddy, to tell Mamma company was coming. Then I stopped. I don't know why, but I thought the figure might be By come to visit me. I wanted to see him, but a part of me felt shy. He had found me half dead out on the prairie, and I wondered what he'd thought when he'd had to carry me back home.

I stood waiting, and it took a while, but then he was closer and I was right. It was By.

I started waving when he was still a long way off, hoping he'd see me before he got to the soddy. I wanted him alone first; I didn't want to share him with Sarah or Nathaniel.

By did see me, and came right up the little hillock beside the graveyard. He was riding his mule—a pretty, small gray creature—and he was grinning, showing the gap between his front teeth. That sweet smile I'd noticed the first day made his whole face light up.

"Hey!" he said. "You're better."

"I am."

"I'm glad!"

He climbed off his mule and threw out his arms. "Isn't it beautiful here?" he said. "Isn't it pretty? I'm so glad you're better!"

I had to smile, the way he looked so happy.

And then I looked around me at the prairie, alive,

shining in the sun, felt the wind blowing softly on us, the sun making my hair hot, and I realized it was a beautiful day. This was a beautiful place. And I was glad that I was—well, alive. Yes, glad to be here.

# Fifteen

BY WAS holding the mule's halter while he looked for a place to tie her up.

"You can use the fence," I said. "What's her name?"

I reached out to pat the mule but suddenly felt too tired. I sat down and leaned back against the fence.

"Cory," he said. He patted her flank, then tied her to the fence, and slid to the ground behind me. "Know what?" he said. "Riding a mule makes your rear end hurt."

I laughed, remembering the day I had told him that.

"Boy, am I glad you're better," he said. "The day I found you, I thought you were dead."

"Well, I'm not!" I said.

"I can see that!" he said. "But that day, you weren't even moving. And know what else? There was a vulture watching you."

"Really?" I said.

"Really!" he said. "Did you know they don't eat you if you're alive? They wait for you to die."

"That's polite of them," I said, meaning to be a bit sarcastic, but By just nodded seriously.

"It is!" he said. "They've got a bad reputation, but they're not really bad, not like wolves or coyotes or bears that eat you up alive."

"Well, I'm glad you found me before the vulture got me," I said. "I don't remember it, though, not any of it."

"That's 'cause you were hardly even breathing. You looked terrible." He snuck a look at me. "I was scared of you," he said quietly.

"Scared?" I said. "Why?"

He shuddered. "Because!" he said. "It's real spooky being near a dead person."

I looked away, heard Mamma's words—"Hold your brother. Say good-bye."

Yes, it was spooky—but that wasn't the worst part.

"Know what my mamma said about you?" By asked.

"What?" I said.

"She says you're a miracle. She says God has a plan for you, that He doesn't want you to die yet, if He let me find you." He tilted his head at me. "You think that's true?" he asked.

I shook my head and thought about what I had said to Papa—that I thought God was dreadful. And Papa said he sometimes agreed. I sighed.

"I don't know," I said. "What do you think?"

By only shrugged. "I don't know. But you know what? We're almost ready to come out here, in about a week. It's real different from where we lived in Dakota, but I'm excited to homestead. I'm going to help build our house. We'll be down that creek in back, not more than five miles."

"My mamma will be happy to have neighbors," I said. "We'll all be happy." I realized then that I didn't know anything about him. "Do you have brothers, sisters?" I asked.

He shook his head. "Just me," he said. "I'm an orphan."

"No," I said. "You can't be an orphan. Not if you have a mamma."

He shrugged. "I used to be an orphan. My mamma died first, and later, my papa died, too, and my papa's family couldn't take me. So my new mamma adopted me. I'm Lakota."

"Indian?" I asked.

By nodded. "My papa wasn't. But my mamma was Lakota. I'm Lakota!"

He said it proudly, and I wondered what it was like to be Indian, or part Indian anyway. I sometimes pretended to be Indian, when I was out alone with Maggie, riding astride her, bareback. I pretended I could run with the wind, and . . . and I was late getting home that day.

I looked at him, waiting, wondering if he'd tell more. But he didn't.

"Do you have cousins or anything?" I asked, finally. "Do your aunts have children?"

Again he shook his head. "No. But you know what?"

I made a face at him. "No, I don't know what!" I said. It came out kind of snappy sounding. That was another thing that had happened about being sick—I felt mad and even mean so much of the time.

But By didn't seem to notice that I was being snappy. He just laughed. "My mamma has plans," he said. "She wants all her students to take part in the July Fourth festival."

"The festival!" I said. "We went last year, and it was such fun! But what do you mean, her students? She doesn't have any yet. I mean there's us, but . . ."

"She knows who they'll be." He went over to Cory and took something out of one of the saddlebags. Then he turned to me, sat down, and handed me an envelope.

"It's a letter to your mamma, but you can read it," he said.

"It's all right to read it?" I said. "You're sure?"

"Why not?" he said. "I did."

I shrugged, then took it out of the envelope.

*Dear Mrs. Chrisman,* the letter said.

*With your permission, I would like your children to take part in a recitation on July*

*Fourth at the festival. I am sure, as you know better than I, it is a lively event, with people coming from miles around. It would make us all proud to see our students perform. I would like them to do a recitation of the Declaration of Independence. We could meet early on the fourth to rehearse, and perform at ten o'clock. I do hope this meets with your approval.*

*I know we will soon be neighbors, and I look forward to calling on you then. And I do send prayers for the complete and speedy recovery of your daughter Abbie.*

*Sincerely,*
*Miss Maude Richardson.*

I took a deep breath, thinking about the festival and about recitations, remembering. At church, back in St. Joseph, we'd had recitations every year—at Christmas, holidays, and festivals. But since we'd come to the prairie, we hadn't taken part in any—only the town children did a pageant at the Fourth of July festival last year. I loved recitations. I felt proud standing up on the stage, with everyone looking at me.

I looked up from the letter and handed it back to By, smiling. "The festival is fun!" I said. "Last year, it went on for two whole days and it was wonderful. There were fireworks that shot up into the sky, all different colors, and they boomed out so loud the ground shook. And there were games for the children and dancing for the grown-ups, and bands and so many people! Someone said there were two thousand people there. And the table with the food—I measured it myself, with a yard ruler Papa gave me—it was a hundred forty feet long! There were horse races and mule races and ox pulls."

"I'll enter Cory in the mule races," By said. "She'll win."

"Last year," I said, "some of the mules wouldn't go anywhere, and some wandered off the course! Mamma said people were betting on the mules. She thought that was dreadful."

By only shrugged. "I'd bet on Cory. She's real fast, and she's never stubborn like other mules. That's because I treat her right. You ever ride a mule?

I shook my head. "No. Just a horse."

"Want to?" he said. "Cory's real gentle. You could try it now."

"Not yet," I said. "I'm still kind of shaky."

"You'll be better by the festival," By said. "You'll be in the recitation."

I suddenly remembered something, and it made a pain come inside me, like something bad had happened to my heart. I took a deep breath and looked away. Land sale. The land sale was held the days of the festival, the same two days. How could I have forgotten?

What was Papa going to do? It was an auction, so if we didn't have the money, someone else might buy out our place. Papa wouldn't be able to bear that.

Or did Papa have the money to buy out? And if he had the money, did he still want to? Did Mamma? I had begun to feel lately that even Mamma was worn down by the prairie. She'd become so silent since Charlie's death, not constantly reminding me of God's presence and His will, not telling me so much to be happy with my lot. Was it because maybe she wasn't so happy with hers?

I had no idea what Mamma or Papa were going to do. I didn't even know anymore what I hoped they would do.

After a bit, I said, "I think maybe we won't be going to the festival."

"Why?" By said. "You said yourself that everybody comes."

I shrugged. I didn't think I could explain, and didn't really want to. "It's hard to explain," I said. "I just don't think we will. So you'll have to tell your mamma I can't take part in her recitation."

By stood up and stretched, then grinned down at me. "You will," he said. "My mamma always gets her way. You wait and see. You'll be there."

# Sixteen

THE FOLLOWING Saturday, Nathaniel took the wagon to town to bring Papa out to us. I wanted to go, too, but Mamma said I wasn't strong enough.

I knew I was shaky, and I still felt quiet—moody, Mamma called it—but I wasn't that weak.

"Please, Mamma," I begged. "What difference does it make if I sit here in the soddy or in a wagon? I'll be fine."

Mamma shook her head.

"Mamma?" Nathaniel said then. "I'll go real slow. And we won't go over ruts or anything."

But again, she shook her head.

I sighed and shrugged, and Nathaniel did, too. We didn't ask again. Once Mamma makes up her mind, there's no arguing with her.

Later, after Nathaniel had been gone awhile,

Mamma turned to me. "I want you to lie down now," she said. "If you want to stay up to see Papa, you need to rest." She squinted up her eyes. "You haven't recovered fast enough to suit me."

"I'm feeling fine," I said.

"Well, lie down anyway," Mamma answered. "You can read the Bible or write in that notebook of yours, but I want you to do it lying down."

I shrugged. Besides, truth to tell, I was tired. Some days, I felt strong and happy, and other days, I felt so weak. And even on the well days, sometimes I fell asleep before supper. It was strange to feel well and happy one day, and to be sad and sick the next. Some days, I still cried.

Now I took my notebook and lay down on my mattress. But lying there, propped on one elbow, I realized I didn't know what to write. I hadn't written a word in weeks.

I looked at Sarah, at Mamma, both of them in front of the little bit of mirror over the table, Mamma brushing out Sarah's hair and braiding it anew.

Sarah was examining herself in the mirror, her little face screwed up, like she was wondering if she had changed since last time she'd looked. Just in the last weeks, I'd noticed that her cheeks were more filled out, and her eyes were clear and shiny, but it wasn't just that she was better and healthier looking. There was something else, maybe the way she carried herself, like she was almost grown-up. I wondered now what she was thinking, if she knew she had changed.

She was chattering to Mamma, talking about wearing her hair up, and then about cutting her hair and letting bits of it fly loose for the birds to put in their nests—chattering away like she used to before she got sick.

"Mamma?" she said now. "Do you think I'm pretty?"

Mamma shook her head. "Pretty is as pretty does," she said, the same thing she'd said to me that one time. But she laughed when she said it, and I could see her give Sarah's hair a tug with the brush.

"But tell me true," Sarah said. "Am I?"

Mamma pulled her lips into a line. "Vanity is the work of the devil," she said.

Sarah sighed. "But tell me, please?" she said. "Just once. Am I? I don't know how to tell if I am or not."

For a minute, Mamma didn't answer. And then she said, "I guess you're pretty enough."

I saw Sarah smile, and I couldn't help smiling, too. That was a big compliment for Mamma.

I was smiling at something else, too—Sarah's question meant she was growing up, inside as well as outside. I remembered when I was like Sarah, always thinking about pretty—if I was or not, what I'd be like when I grew up. Now, I felt like pretty didn't matter so much anymore. Well, it did, but other things seemed more important now.

"Abbie?" Sarah said, seeing me watching her. "Do you think I'm pretty?"

"Now that's enough about pretty," Mamma said.

I smiled at Sarah. "I think so," I said. "I think you're very pretty."

Sarah stared at herself for a long moment. And then she said, "Mamma?" She sounded hesitant, a little anxious. "Mamma, can I ask you something?"

"If it's not more vanity," Mamma said.

"It's not. Mamma, is Charlie an angel now?"

Mamma pulled the brush through Sarah's hair. "I believe so, child," she said quietly.

"I'm glad, Mamma," Sarah said. "I want him to be an angel, a beautiful angel. And there are no snakes in heaven, right?"

Mamma didn't answer for a while, and Sarah looked over at me.

"No snakes," I said softly.

And then Mamma answered, her voice sounding tired, "They say there are no bad things in heaven."

"I'm glad," Sarah said, sighing. "He's happy, and he's beautiful, and he'll always be beautiful. A beautiful angel."

Mamma didn't answer, and I hoped Sarah wouldn't say any more. I knew talking about Charlie made Mamma sad.

It made me sad, too. I lay back on the mattress and closed my eyes. I could hear Mamma and Sarah talking about Papa coming home, and it was reassuring, comforting somehow, to feel us here together, all of us looking forward to Papa's return. I breathed deep, felt my breath coming slow, easy, that soft, quiet way it does before sleep.

I used to try and hold on to that time—that half-sleep, half-wake time. Now, though, I liked slipping off to sleep.

I think I slept a little bit then, or maybe I was still just drifting off, but I suddenly heard my name.

"I'm not sure Abbie wants to go to the festival," Mamma was saying. Her voice was low, but I could hear her plain enough. "She hasn't said a word. But I know you want to, and so does Nathaniel, and we'll just have to wait and see what your papa has to say when he comes home. I'll give Miss Richardson a definite answer then."

"But, Mamma?" Sarah said. "Everybody's going, and Miss Richardson really wants us to be in the recitation. And you know how much fun the festival was last year! I think it would be good for Abbie. I think she'd love it."

"Who knows what Abbie would like?" Mamma said. "So quiet, she is. And something strange? I never thought I'd say this, but I miss her constant chatter."

"She was really sick, wasn't she?" Sarah said.

"Nathaniel was, too," Mamma said. "But see how fast he's recovered."

"But he wasn't as sick as Abbie, was he?"

"No," Mamma said. "No, he wasn't."

There was a silence, then, and I made my breathing slower, easy and deep, not wanting them to know I was listening.

I head Mamma sigh—even from across the soddy

I could hear her breath whoosh out in the way she has when she's really troubled.

"I just wonder what goes on in Abbie's head," Mamma said. "Wonder what's troubling her."

But Mamma did know what went on in my head. She hadn't said a word about it, but she knew. She knew I'd been out on the prairie, playing, being addle-brained, talking to antelope, not thinking, not coming back to fetch the doctor in time. She must know!

And she knew the other worries, too.

"Maybe it's just that she misses Charlie?" Sarah said, her voice small.

Mamma sighed again, and I could picture her, passing her hand over her forehead, rubbing her eyes. "We all do, child," she said. "God knows, we all do."

"Anyway," Sarah said, "Papa's coming home soon! And he'll tell us about the festival, and maybe we'll go and play games and everything."

"Maybe so," Mamma answered. "Now help me get the cookstove lit up. We've spent enough time sitting and chatting like ladies of leisure."

I heard her chair scrape back, and Sarah's, too, and I breathed deep, a sleeping kind of breath, and another, slow and deep. And then, they must have been real sleeping breaths, because I dreamed that Charlie was there, rolling 'round and 'round on a mattress on the ground, while I was up somewhere, like on a balcony above him. He was rolling over and over like he always did, like a baby raccoon, but he was a raccoon with wings, and they got in the way when he rolled over. I reached down to help him, but the balcony was too high and I couldn't reach him no matter how hard I tried.

And then, next thing I knew, Papa was at the door to the soddy, Nathaniel behind him, and Mamma and Sarah were crowding around them. Then Papa came in and he was smiling down at me, reaching for me, and I sat up, smiled back, and reached out my arms to him.

Papa was home.

# Seventeen

WE ATE a late supper, sitting on the ground outside the soddy, like we were at a picnic. It was an awfully hot night, and the soddy felt like an oven. After my nap, I was dripping with sweat, and the small breeze outside was welcome.

Nathaniel had had luck with his shooting that morning, and Mamma had roasted the prairie chicken in the cookstove. There was bread, too, and radishes and beans from the garden, and Mamma had made a bread pudding with berries—a regular feast.

When we were all finished, and Sarah and Mamma had cleaned up the dishes and pans, Papa brought out the New Testament, and in the waning light, he began to read to us.

I leaned back against the soddy, and Nathaniel settled down close to me. He took my hand, holding it the way Sarah sometimes does, something he rarely did before we both got sick.

He smiled at me as Papa began to read, and I looked back at him, thinking how the summer sun had changed him. His arms and hands were tanned and freckled, his eyebrows even lighter from the sun, and his face was a mass of freckles, especially across his nose. But his smile was always the same—sweet.

I smiled at him, then looked up at the darkening sky, then around at the rest of my family. Mamma seemed peaceful, in spite of the sad lines around her eyes that had come since Charlie died. Sarah was lying next to Papa, her head in his lap, her breathing slow and deep, and I had a feeling she'd be asleep in minutes.

Papa read aloud, from Luke: " 'He who is not with me is against me, and he who does not gather with me scatters.' "

He read for a long time, and I put my head back against the soddy, my eyes closed, listening.

" 'When the unclean spirit has gone out of a man,' " Papa read, " 'he roams through waterless places in search of a resting place, and finding none, he says, "I will return to my house which I left." And when he has come, he finds the place swept and . . .' "

I opened my eyes, looked at Mamma again, and saw her head nodding low, like she was falling asleep just like Sarah had. Even Nathaniel's hand was growing heavy in mine.

After a few more minutes of reading, Papa stopped, looked around at Mamma, Sarah, and Nathaniel, and looked at me. "Seems you and I are the only ones listening to the word of God," he said softly, smiling at me.

I smiled back. "That's because I slept all afternoon," I answered quietly.

"I'm going to put your brother and sister on their beds," Papa said. "Then how about you and me, we walk a short ways? There should be star showers tonight. Maybe we'll be lucky and see them."

"All right," I said.

I sat and watched as Papa touched Mamma's shoulder, awakening her, and then awakening Nathaniel. They all went into the soddy, Mamma first, then Papa carrying Sarah, Nathaniel stumbling along behind.

After a few minutes, Papa came back out, a lantern in his hand, but he hadn't lit the lantern, for there was still enough light in the sky. "Ready?" he said.

I nodded and stood up, and he reached for my hand.

We walked away from the soddy, not toward Grand Island, but the other way, as though we were going further onto the plains, out where people said it was just a desert.

We walked quite a while, and then I turned around and looked back. From where we were, there was no sign of the soddy, no sign of any life out here, the plains still and empty. There were no sounds, either, not a bird or an owl or even a cricket. The only noise came from our own feet and the small, *snick, snick* sound of the lantern swinging softly in Papa's hand.

I heard Papa breathe in, that soft sound he does so often, like a deep sigh. He always smiles after he breathes like that, and it makes me think that he's letting go of something, some trouble or worry.

He turned, smiled at me. "It's a good place to be, isn't it?" he said. "I love it here in spite of everything."

"It's good to be with you," I said.

"Look!" Papa said then, pointing to the sky. "The first star, the evening star. Make a wish."

I remembered that night riding back from town, how I'd wished for Charlie and Nathaniel. How I'd wished for my brothers to be well.

Tonight I didn't wish. Wishing was a child's game. But I didn't tell Papa that.

Above us, more stars began to wink on. After a while, the sky was filled with them, stars hanging so low it seemed we could walk right into them, a tangle of them almost at our feet.

"What beauty!" Papa said.

We walked on, and after a while, we came to a low ridge, a place where Sarah and Nathaniel and I played in winter. There, the land rolled a bit, and you could see into the distance. We always pretended it was a real hill, and we were on the lookout for Indians.

Sometimes we saw them, too.

"Shall we sit?" Papa said.

I nodded.

We sat side by side, both of us looking up at the sky. I pulled my knees up and wrapped my arms around them. I didn't see any shooting stars yet, but the night sky and the stars were beautiful.

After a few minutes, Papa said, "Know what I think of when I look at the stars?"

"What, Papa?" I said.

"Well," Papa said. "You know how the stars are up there all the time, even in daytime, but you just can't see them?"

I nodded. "I know that, Papa," I said.

"Well," Papa said, "seems to me that's how it is with God. He's always there. Sometimes we see His workings, and other times—well, we can't see. Or we only see the bad things, storms and clouds and rain. But God's always there, just behind those things, just like the stars are always there."

I nodded, but I didn't answer. I didn't understand God, not at all. I didn't understand God being there and not seeing Him. I didn't understand Him having a plan for me like By's mamma said. And Mamma and Sarah saying Charlie was an angel—well, if God wanted angels, why couldn't he just make Himself some angels? Why did He need Charlie?

But I could say none of this to Papa.

We were quiet a while longer, and then Papa slid an arm around my shoulder, pulling me close. "Can I tell you a story?" he said. "I've been thinking about it all week. Would you like to hear?"

"What kind of story?" I said.

"It's a once-upon-a-time story," Papa answered. "All right?"

"All right," I said.

"Once upon a time," Papa said, and I could hear the smile in his voice. "Once upon a time I had a daughter. She was wonderfully bright and quick and funny. She laughed and she played, and she had this wonderful mind, full of ideas and imaginations, full of dreams and wishes. She was brilliant, that's what she was, and she dreamed dreams and she was—irrepressible. Nothing got her down, not for long. Yes, that's the kind of daughter she was." He stopped, took a deep breath. "Recognize her?" he asked.

I shrugged, but I smiled. "Sort of," I said.

"Well," Papa went on, and his voice got low, sad sounding, "one day, some bad things happened to her, very bad, and . . . and she changed. She got sad and she went away." Papa sighed, looked at me. "And I don't know where she went."

"She didn't go away," I said. "You're being silly. She's still here."

"I don't think so," Papa said. "I think she's gone, and I miss her. I want her back. And I'll do whatever it takes to get her back. If I knew where she went, what made her sad, why . . ."

No, no he didn't want to know why—he'd hate me just like Mamma hated me. And yet, this afternoon, when I was supposed to be sleeping, Mamma didn't seem to hate me.

I swallowed hard. "You don't want to know."

"Oh, I do," Papa said. "And, Abbie . . ."

He turned, held me by the shoulders, looking at me in the moonlight. "Abbie," he said, "if it's the prairie, if it means leaving here, then we can probably manage that."

"No!" I said. "It's not that. It's . . ."

"Charlie," Papa said softly.

I nodded, and then I started to cry. "Charlie's dead!" I said. "And it's all my fault. It's that stupid girl you were talking about. She plays, and you know what she was doing that day, when she was supposed to go straight home? She was riding on Maggie's back, wearing Nathaniel's trousers, that's what she was doing. And then she stopped to daydream and talk to antelopes! Can you believe that, talk to antelopes! And . . . and she fell asleep and it was too late when she got home. And now Charlie's dead. And she's gone. And good riddance. And God doesn't even care!"

"Oh, my dear," Papa said. "Oh, my dear, dear girl."

"I'm not a dear girl, I'm a bad girl. And—"

And then I couldn't talk—the tears were choking my throat.

Papa pulled me in, held me close, held me tight while I cried and cried. And after a bit, I sat up, wiped my face on my apron, and then I cried some more. Then Papa gave me a piece of his shirttail, and I cried into that, too. For a long time Papa held me while I cried. Until, at last, the tears were done.

# Eighteen

WHEN I was quiet again, Papa said, "Seems to me you've got it wrong. Don't you know that?"

I sat up, wiped my eyes again. "How?" I said. "How do I have it wrong?"

Papa said, "Don't you know Charlie died in Mamma's arms, the doctor doing everything he could, and still Charlie died. The doctor was right there. And Nathaniel got the same treatment, the same doctor, and yet he didn't die. And you didn't, either."

"But if I'd come back sooner . . ."

"No, my dear!" Papa said. "That's not true."

"How do you know?" I said.

Papa sighed. "I know. You must trust me," he said. "See, it wasn't a matter of time, nor a matter of how soon the doctor got there. Charlie was just too small. Babies often die of cholera. Bigger people, they have a better chance."

I took a deep breath, long and trembly.

"But how do you know?" I said. "How do you know for sure?"

Papa stood up then and took my hand. "Some things I know, and this is one of them. Other things, there are no answers for. Like why babies die in the first place."

Well, that was true. But was it possible that Papa was right, that Charlie would have died anyway? Papa never says what he does not mean.

"Let's get on home now," Papa said. "The others will be waiting."

We turned and walked on toward home, neither of us saying much, but it was a nice kind of quiet—comfortable, safe—maybe because for the first time since Charlie had died, I didn't have a pain in my heart. As we walked, I kept thinking about what Papa said, what I said, about Charlie, about God, about things that had no answers. But I also thought about other questions, questions that did have answers—should have answers: Us. The land sale. The prairie.

Just before we came to the rise that led to our soddy, I looked over at Papa. "Papa?" I said.

"Yes?" he said.

I took a deep breath. "Are we going to the festival?" I asked.

"Would you like to?" Papa said.

"Maybe," I said. "I think so."

"Just think so?" Papa said.

"Yes, I think so," I said.

"I hear the teacher wants you to do a recitation," Papa said. "Nathaniel told me about it."

"Yes," I said. "But Mamma said she doesn't know if we'll go or not."

"I know," Papa said quietly. "It's a decision we have to make tonight. Tomorrow, at the latest."

He didn't say more, and we walked on till we were right up by the soddy, right outside our fence. And then, I couldn't stand it any longer.

I took a deep breath. "Papa!" I said. "It's land sale time at the festival. And, Papa, I don't know what you're going to do!"

I had said it.

Papa stopped and rested both hands on the fence around our yard. He looked around, looked at the soddy. "Your mamma and me, we're deciding," he said quietly.

"What do you mean?" I said.

Papa turned his head to look toward the line of scraggly trees along the stream in back, but he didn't look at me. "What do you wish for?" he asked.

"I . . . don't know," I said. "I don't even know if you have the money."

"It will be close," Papa said. "It's an auction, but they almost never go above a dollar twenty-five an acre for people who are already on the land. If the auction stays at one twenty-five, we can just about do it."

I took a deep breath. "Then that's what we're doing?" I said. "Staying?"

For a long time, Papa didn't answer. And then he said only, "I love the prairie. And Mamma and me, we love the opportunities it gives us."

"Oh," I said.

"But," Papa said, "you haven't told me yet what you hope for."

I looked away from him, out to the prairie, up at the sky, at the stars hanging above us, around us, in front of us. I heard the breeze whispering to us and, off somewhere, the sound of a coyote—or a wolf maybe—announcing its presence. And underneath it all, the sound of silence, prairie silence, the still sound of the night.

What did I want? What did I hope for? I didn't know. And then, I felt my heart beating wildly because I did know. I did. I wanted both. I wanted to live in town. And I wanted to stay on the prairie.

Papa turned to me then, his eyebrows up. "Yes?" he said.

"Both!" I said. "I want both."

Papa smiled. "And if you can't have both?"

"I don't know!" I said. "I shouldn't have to make this decision. I'm just a child!"

Papa laughed then. He reached out and hugged me to him so hard the breath whooshed out of me. He held me away from him, smiled down at me. "Irrepressible!" he said. "My irrepressible girl is back. But, my dear, I'm not asking you to make that decision. I'm asking what it is you wish."

Again, I looked away.

Across the yard, I could see the soddy, see the lamplight shining from the single window. I knew that inside, Mamma was resting, fighting sleep, so she could wait for Papa, be encircled by his arms. I knew that Nathaniel was in there, too, asleep in his corner bed, and Sarah was sprawled across our mattress, taking the whole space. And under my part of the mattress were my writing book, my personal things. And by the hearth was the candy I'd bought that day, still waiting for a celebration so we could eat it.

And there was an empty place by the fireplace, where Charlie used to be.

I thought of all those things, and thought—it's home. And the Richardsons were coming, neighbors, and By was coming, and we'd have a schoolteacher, a real one. It was different from St. Joseph. But it was home.

I looked up at Papa and took a deep breath. "Just a minute!" I said. "Wait?"

He frowned at me, but before he could open his mouth or say a single word, I ran from his side across the yard in the moonlight. I tiptoed into the soddy, saw Mamma still awake on her bed, saw her sit up and frown at me.

"It's all right," I whispered.

I went to my mattress, reached under it, and took something out. "Be right back," I said.

Then, I ran back outside, across the yard to where Papa still waited by the fence.

"Here, Papa!" I said, and I put something in his hand. "It's for you. In case you need it. In case the auction goes higher."

Papa looked down at it—at my wishing bag filled with money that I'd put into his hand—then back at me. Even in the moonlight I could see tears shimmer in his eyes.

"In case you don't have quite enough," I said. "It's for you. I mean, it's for us."

# Epilogue

SUMMER HAS come and gone, and fall, too, and the golden fields of grass all are withered and dried now, making cricking, snapping sounds in the wind as we all wait for the first snows. The geese have come to peck the fields, and the sand cranes have flown over on their way south. The whooping cranes are gone, too. I saw the whooping cranes dance that day, the day of the festival, the day Papa was able to buy our land, to become a real landowner.

I had left the festival after the recitation—and what a wonderful recitation it was. By and I had gone down to the river looking for Crazy Annie. When we got there, there was no Annie. But there were whooping cranes.

There were twelve of them on the island, tall and white, I counted them, their wings fluttering, heads bent as though they were praying. They began to form a circle, two in the middle, the others ringed around them. And then, as we watched, the birds began to dance. The ones on the outside began moving, 'round and 'round in a circle, making a kind of wild sound, halfway between a cry and a wild chant. The ones in the middle moved faster, faster, bowing their heads into their white breasts, bowing and lifting, heads up and down, then one foot up, then down, up and down, high-stepping in the way I'd seen fancy horses do.

I held my breath, watching, hardly daring to breathe. The whooping cranes went on and on, fluttering their wings, dancing for one another, a solemn ritual that we couldn't understand.

Above us, the sky was brilliant blue, and the grasses waved about us. I had never seen such a thing, never, and I will never forget it. Not even the antelope was as beautiful.

It's one of the many prairie things I'm writing about now. I'm also writing about our family, in St. Joseph and on the prairie, writing in my notebooks, filling up book after book. Papa keeps buying me new ones, and Miss Richardson says I will be a good writer someday. She says one needs to write, to practice. But she says one needs something more—one needs to have something important to say in order to be a writer. She says I have important things to say. So now every night, I take my notebook and candle into this little room Papa is building, off to the side of the soddy, because I like to be alone when I write. It is cold in here, no fire yet, but it's a perfect, private place to write. Each morning I share what I have written with Miss Richardson.

Sarah and Nathaniel and I go to school each day to Miss Richardson's—three miles' walk along the creek and three miles back. Probably when the snows get real heavy, we won't go, but for now, we do. There are seven more children there, who come from the other side of Grand Island. All in all, we are a happy group, and I know Mamma is relieved when I tell her that. It eases her to know I'm finally happy with my lot.

Mamma and Papa seem happy, too, and the new baby, Maria, has come to join us, and she is the happiest baby ever.

But the best thing has happened just today, and that is what I need to write about tonight. Because I learned something today, something big. I was out on the prairie with Maggie, collecting buffalo chips in the wagon, and I chanced to look up, and there, all alone in the sky, I saw a whooping crane. It wasn't with a flock, and I wondered for a minute if it had gotten lost, separated from its family, until I saw another join up and there were two—maybe making their own little family, just the two of them. But looking at them in that cold, gray sky, a sky laden with coming snow, I suddenly began thinking about something Papa had said last summer.

Stars. There were stars up there. Looking skyward at all those leaden gray clouds, I remembered that there were stars hidden there. I suddenly knew it. I mean—I didn't just know it in my head, I knew it inside me, deep inside, I *knew* it. And I knew, too, that it wasn't only stars—or even God—that Papa had been talking about that day. He meant that there's always good hiding somewhere, even if you can't see it. And there is. Like us here, having our home on the prairie.

When Maria gets bigger and can understand words, it's the first thing I will tell her. I will have her look up at the sky and tell her about the stars. She might not believe at first—because she'll be too little—but she'll learn from me, her big sister: The stars are always there.

# A Note About This Book

IN THE Nebraska of the late 1850s, land could be acquired through land sales, after "proving out." To prove out, one had to be male or the head of a household, and had to prove that he was living on the land and had built a house at least twelve feet by fourteen feet, that the house had a window, and also that a well had been dug. If that had been accomplished, there was a land sale, usually once a year, at which time one had to pay for the land, the amount usually being about a dollar and twenty-five cents an acre. This sale was nominally an auction, yet seldom did anyone have to pay more than a dollar twenty-five if he was already occupying the land. Later, in 1862, the Homestead Act became law, which said that anyone, male or female, who was the head of a household or who had attained the age of twenty-one was entitled to one hundred sixty acres of land.

Many families began their lives on the prairie in sod houses. These were homes made of blocks of sod dug out of the earth, then placed one atop another to build walls and a roof. Sometimes the roof was supported by branches of cottonwood trees, then covered over with a final layer of sod. These houses were dark and hard to keep clean, since dust and dirt and bugs often fell from the walls and roof onto the inhabitants.

In those years, the prairie was a dangerous place for settlers. Indian bands were occasionally violent, hungry as they were, having lost many of their hunting lands. Loneliness and hardship and disease also took their tolls among the settlers. Cholera was particularly prevalent, and many settlers succumbed to this as well as to smallpox, influenza, and other virulent illnesses. There were also real and constant dangers presented by the land—snakes, wolves, and other wildlife being a constant and sometimes bitter challenge.

This story takes place in the Nebraska of the late 1850s, in the area around Grand Island along the Platte River in eastern Nebraska, before the Homestead Act.